WALL STREET JOURNAL & USA TODAY
BESTSELLING AUTHOR
KB WINTERS

Copyright and Disclaimer

This book is a work of fiction. The names, characters, places and incidents are products of the writer's imagination and have been used fictitiously and are not to be construed as real. Any resemblance to persons, living or dead, actual events, locales or organizations is entirely coincidental.

Copyright © 2017 Book Boyfriends Publishing

All rights reserved. No part of this publication may be reproduced, stored in or introduced into a retrieval system, or transmitted, in any form, or by any means (electronic, mechanical, photocopying, recording, or otherwise) without the prior written permission of the copyright owner. The author acknowledges the trademarked status and trademark owners of various products referenced in this work of fiction, which have been used without permission. The publication/use of the trademarks is not authorized, associated with, or sponsored by the trademark owners.

Table of Contents

Copyright and Disclaimer i

Prologue 1

Chapter One 7

Chapter Two 25

Chapter Three 45

Chapter Four 59

Chapter Five 67

Chapter Six 83

Chapter Seven 101

Chapter Eight 117

Chapter Nine 133

Epilogue... 149

MICK

CAOS MC (BOOK ONE)

By KB Winters

MICK

Prologue

Talon *– One month ago*

My father was dead. To be fair, I thought my dad had been dead all of my twenty-three years because that was what my mom had told me. She said he died before I was born and had no family. So, it had always been just the two of us. Mom and me against the world. No father for me unless you count mom's string of boyfriends who had no use for a curious little girl in need of male attention.

Obviously, that was all a lie because I finally sat down with the baby faced lawyer in the expensive blue suit who'd been hounding me for weeks to learn that my father had actually died less than a year ago. Nine months to be exact. How could I not feel it? How could I not know that while I wished and prayed for some kind of family as my mom lay dying in the cancer ward, someone else had been out there? He'd been looking for me my whole life.

And only months after his death had he succeeded. *Damn.* Actually, the lawyer told me a friend of my dad felt compelled to finish the search after his death and that right there turned me into a hot mess of emotions because that kind of friendship was rare. Special.

I had so many mixed up thoughts and feelings about all the information that had just been dumped on me, and I just sat on the wall overlooking Lake Michigan to try and clear my mind. Sometimes the cool breeze off the water helped, but I had a feeling nothing could help me now. And the worst part about it? My mom wasn't here anymore, so I couldn't ask her why she kept me from him. Why she denied me a father. I didn't know if I wanted to scream, puke or cry.

At first, I thought maybe she'd been afraid of him, but as I remembered the things she'd told me—

MICK

he fixed motorcycles, had a great laugh, played the guitar like a pro—I realized that she still loved him. Even years after fleeing and hiding from him, she loved him. *So why, Mom?*

Sliding off the wall, I made my way back to the parking garage a few blocks away and decided I'd give my boyfriend, Damon, a chance to help me figure things out. According to the lawyer, my dad Magnus Ashbee—funny how we still had the same last name—spent the past thirty years in a small California town along the Mexican border called Brently. He owned a house on a few acres of land plus a diner, and now it was all mine.

If I was ready to step up and claim it.

By the time I made it home, I was no closer to a decision. I couldn't deny a certain amount of interest about my dad's life all these years. Did he have a wife or other children? Did I have brothers and sisters? Was he happy? Did he hate Mom for hiding from him all these years? The curiosity burned in my gut with the need to know.

I probably should've been paying more attention because I didn't even notice my best friend Abby's car in the drive, though her teal hobo bag lay across the sofa and her laughter rang out from the kitchen. With a smile at the laughter I heard, I shrugged off my jacket and hung it up then followed the laughter. *No, not the laughter* I corrected as my eyes settled on the scene before me. *Giggles*. Abby was fucking giggling. With her bare legs wrapped around Damon's waist while he sank his cock inside her.

"Guess you weren't expecting me home so soon."

Both of the lying, cheating cowards froze. Probably worried about how I might react. "Talon, babe let me explain. Shit!" Damon gave me that slick salesman smile that I fucking loathed. In that moment, I hated it more than I ever had.

I pushed my palm into the air and pinched my eyes closed, tamping down the fury of rage that fired through me. I heard the unmistakable sound of

MICK

bodies untangling and forced my eyes open as Damon pulled out of Abby. Raw, I might add. "I'm not really interested in anything you have to say. Put your dick away and get out. Both of you."

Abby slid off my kitchen table with her bare ass and stood in front of me, contrition shining in her traitorous green eyes. "Talon, we just got carried away—ow! What the fuck?" Now anger shone, and I dared her to retaliate, to give me a reason to give her the beat down she really fucking deserved.

Yeah, I'm not ashamed to say I slapped the shit out of her. "I don't give a shit what you have to say, you rotten skank. Get the fuck out and don't come back." When she didn't move fast enough I pushed her, causing her head to slam against the wall. I had zero fucks left to give. "Go!"

"Talon baby, calm down. It was just a mistake." Damon smiled that pop star grin, a flop of blond hair hanging over one eye.

I smiled at him and cupped his jaw. He really was a beautiful man with blond hair and clear baby blue eyes, but apparently, he had a slippery cock, and I didn't share. "I doubt it was a mistake," I told him as I raked my nails down his left cheek. "And I doubt it was the first time. What's more—I don't give a fuck. Get out, and don't come back," my voice tremored with anger.

"Ow, you crazy bitch! My face!" He held his cheek as blood trickled to the surface, and I smiled proudly. It'll be hard for him to go into the office tomorrow with those marks on his pretty little face. "I'll be back when you've calmed down," he tossed over his shoulder as he strolled out of our apartment. Our *former* apartment, I amended.

I didn't bother with a response because those two—the closest thing I had to family—had helped me make the decision I'd been struggling with for the past two hours.

Looked like I was going to Brently.

MICK

Chapter One

Mick

It was another fuckin' beautiful day, and I should have been out on my bike letting the warm breeze brush my skin as the sun shone on my back. Instead, I was leaning against the house that used to belong to my mentor, my surrogate father, and my club brother. Magnus Ashbee had been gone for almost nine months, and I missed that old man more than I thought possible. Something about his death had left my guts churning with a desperate need to find the truth, and I'd figure it out. No matter what. Magnus was a decorated Navy SEAL. The man had done more covert operations than anyone I knew. He'd seen so much shit, it had changed him, made him realize who the real enemy was.

CAOS Five was actually started in the seventies by Vietnam vets. They were responsible for ridding the area of drugs permanently. Even before the fucking War on Drugs and before crack decimated whole neighborhoods and then meth, they had taken on drug traffickers, cartels, and gangs looking to get rich on the suffering of others. Now the rest of us continued their legacy. We did our own shit, mostly bikes, guns, and girls, but that shit never included drugs. Ever.

Figuring out the truth behind Magnus' death was for another day, though, because I didn't come by to stroll down memory lane. I stood out here waiting for the kid Magnus had never been able to find after two decades of searching. Going through his things after we put him in the ground, I knew I had to finish what he'd started. It had taken some time, but we'd found her. *Talon*. What a sexy ass name.

She stepped from the cute little red SUV, showing off shapely legs covered in short shorts and

MICK

punctuated with those little wedge sandals with big loopy ribbons around the ankles. When she straightened, I saw she was a tiny thing, probably just over five feet, but enough curves to keep a hungry man satisfied. And dammit, I was starving. The red and white sleeveless blouse she wore tied at the waist gave her a Midwestern farm girl appeal that made my cock stand up and pay attention. *Get it together, man, she's Magnus' daughter.* "You Talon?"

She turned at the sound of my voice, silver eyes as wide as saucers. "Y-y-yep."

She's afraid of me. My lips curled up at that thought. Most women bent over backward and offered all kind of sexual depravity just for a night with me, and this little thing stuttered at the sight of me. "I don't bite, darlin', unless you ask me to." I chuckled at the way pink rose up her bare skin.

She laughed, and damn that husky sound was another arrow of lust between my legs. "I'm not afraid, it's just I've never seen someone like you in real life." She reached forward, about to touch one of the tats on my arm, but she pulled back at the last minute. *Damn.* "You're so big. And colorful," she said, eyes again straying to the ink covering my arms. Then she licked her lips, and I wanted to believe there was desire in her eyes, but I couldn't be sure.

I groaned and took a step back, forcing myself to remember who she was. "I guess all this was a pretty big surprise?" I motioned to the house and the land.

She nodded and explained that the lawyer had given her a couple letters written by Magnus. "My mom always told me he had died before I was born." Her voice went wobbly, and I froze. Like most men, I couldn't handle a woman crying. "Did you know him well? Was he a good man?"

I knew what she was asking because the world had exactly one view of motorcycle clubs. Thought they were gangsters, criminals, and all around outlaw assholes. Not CAOS. Sure, we were outlaws, but we had a code of honor. "Magnus was one of the best men I've ever known."

MICK

"Really? How'd you meet him?" I stared at her ass for minute when she bent over to reach for a couple bags before remembering my manners.

I took the bags from her hands and led her inside, continuing, "Well, when I left the Navy, I had no idea what I wanted to do next, so I spent some time riding up and down the coast." I couldn't believe I was opening up to her so easily, but she was as easy to talk to as her dad had been. I took a long drag off my cigarette and continued, "I guess you could've called me a beach bum. I had plenty of money saved up and even if I didn't, I didn't have a desire to *do* anything. So, I took odd jobs just to break up the boredom." I let out a chuckle. "One day my bike sputtered to a stop in the middle of the desert. Next town was fifty miles either way, and then I heard the roar of bikes. It was CAOS."

Her brows bunched in confusion. "CAOS?"

"California Outlaw Sentinel. The club. Anyway, they stopped and your dad got my bike running long enough to get me back to town. We had a few drinks, hit it off and the next thing I know, I'm getting my cut."

She turned her attention back on me from checking out the unfamiliar space, and her gray eyes smiled in my direction. "And they became your family."

I couldn't believe she understood. "More than that, they gave me a purpose when I was at loose ends. But yeah, Magnus was like a father to me and I knew he wanted you here, taking care of two things that meant the world to him. This place and the diner."

"I'm glad you did. I never got a chance to thank you for giving me a piece of him…oh my God! I didn't get your name. It's like I completely forgot my manners."

Damn, she was as adorable as she was sexy. "Mick."

MICK

She took my hand which pretty much swallowed hers whole. "Nice to meet you, Mick. And thank you for this."

"My pleasure." I held her hand a little longer than I needed to, but she felt so damn soft. And she smelled like sunshine and honeysuckle.

Her mouth curled into a smile, those bee-stung lips tantalizing all on their own but with the glittery shiny shit on them—I couldn't help but think about them wrapped around my cock. "I'd ask what you're thinking right now, but I'm not sure I'm ready to hear it."

I loved a girl with a sense of humor, and this chick seemed to have it in spades. Instead of throwing herself at me, she just talked.

"When you're ready, I'll be happy to share."

She cocked her head to the side and gave me a small smile. Then she did the craziest thing, she doubled over with laughter. Her little body shook, and the husky laugh echoed in Magnus' cavernous living room. "You know, Mick, I think I will." She looked around the place again, and I wondered what she saw. An aging home with mismatched furniture? Or did she just see a home? "I didn't intend for you to help me unload my stuff, but I appreciate the help. Can I buy you dinner as thanks? Wait, is there a place to eat this late in a small town?"

"Did you just offer to buy me dinner?" I scraped my hands over my beard and shook my head. Not once in my life had a woman bought me a meal or a drink. Other than my mother, of course.

Talon froze, mouth open in shock. "Shit, sorry. You have a girlfriend who'd have a problem with it. No problem, just point me toward the food, and maybe I'll just send you a six pack instead." Shaking her head and mumbling to herself, she walked to the kitchen and began typing into her phone. "At least he's faithful," she muttered to herself.

"Talon?"

She jumped at the sound of my voice and whirled around. "Yeah?"

MICK

"What are you doing?"

"Creating a shopping list, why?"

"I thought you were buying dinner, or was that just a line?" I wondered if she had as much fight in her as I thought she did.

"I thought...but you said?" She stumbled over her words, tilting her head as she looked at me. She looked confused, but that look faded really quick. "Yes, I'm buying dinner." She straightened and shot me a sweet Midwestern smile then disappeared down the hall. When she returned, she wore a prim little cotton dress that should have turned me off, but damn if I didn't feel my cock harden behind my zipper. "You don't have a girlfriend, right? Because I don't want to start any crap in a new town."

"Completely and totally single. You interested?"

"I might be. Haven't decided yet. Ready?" She winked.

Damn she was feisty. "Always." I grabbed the helmet Magnus kept by the door and watched as Talon locked up. "Put this on."

"But I have my car."

"It'll still be here when we get back. Unless you're scared of a motorcycle," I teased.

Just as I suspected, she snatched the helmet and put it on. "I'm not scared, but what if I were?"

"Then we'd be taking your car." A slow smile spread on her lips as she followed me out to my bike.

"A little help?" She motioned to the bike, and I slid on first.

"Push off me and swing your leg around. And don't forget, Talon, hold on tight."

***

Talon

Sweet hot damn! I'd never been on a motorcycle before, but the ride was exhilarating. Thrilling. My whole body hummed, probably from all

MICK

the vibrations between my legs, but maybe it had a bit to do with the tall, bearded redhead I had been wrapped around for the past fifteen minutes. "That was amazing!"

He grinned back at me in that sexy, kind of restrained way that screamed *trouble*. The best kind of trouble, but trouble nonetheless. Mick was tall—at least six feet four by my estimate—wide and tattooed. I should have been terrified. But I'd seen how sweet he could be, and that left me intrigued. "First time on a bike?"

"Did that classy dismount give away my secret?" I didn't know how laughing had come so easily given everything that had happened lately, but maybe the weeks I took driving across the country were more therapeutic than I realized. "Oh!" My legs wobbled and I nearly fell flat on my face, but Mick's strong arms wrapped around my waist and caught me. "Thank you. Nice arms."

He did that quirk of his lips that almost appeared to be a smile, but not quite. The man had hidden depths, that much was for sure. "Don't know really, too busy checking out your legs." Without another word, he guided me into the diner where apparently, everyone knew his name because we were met with cries of, "Mick!"

"Popular guy," I muttered, wondering if I had another player on my hands. I really hoped not because this man's presence did things to my body that no man had in real life, never mind actual proximity. Not that I had a string of lovers in my past, just Damon and the cliché I lost my virginity to at prom, but until meeting Mick, I would have said that I wasn't a very sexual person.

He guided me to a booth in the back, his big hand splayed across my lower back. "This is a small town, darlin', everyone's popular by default. You plan on sticking around Brently?"

"That's the plan so far. I guess it depends on how things turn out." Though I'd left Chicago pretty much in a hurry, I had a few weeks of driving across the country and talking to myself to really think about my options, and I'd decided to give Brently a fair shot. "This town is kind of small for an all-night diner, isn't it?" I asked as I scooted into the booth.

"Not all night, just open until midnight then reopens at four in time for the truckers to eat and get back on the road."

I sat back and took a moment to really soak him in. Fiery red hair in a short spiky style that should have made him seem less intimidating and a close-cropped beard that he obviously took great care of covered a full set of pink lips and if I had to guess, also a razor-sharp jaw. His eyes seemed bluer because of the red hair and when he looked at me, they smoldered. "Makes sense."

The silence that settled over us was broken by a busty blonde in tight jeans and a pink t-shirt with the words BLACK BETTY scrolled across the chest in large gothic letters. "Hiya, Mick." She leaned over so her tits were just inches from his face, a salacious grin on her red painted mouth. "What can I getcha?"

"Janine. I'll have a Guinness. What do you want, Talon?"

Damn, he'd just straight up ignored what she so clearly offered. I wondered if it was for my benefit or if he really had no interest in her. "I'll have the same. And a burger, medium rare and sweet potato fries."

Mick flashed a grin and then looked up at Janine. "Make it two." He'd been about to say something, but we were interrupted once again by an older woman with salt and pepper hair and an all-black ensemble. "Hey, Charlie, come and meet Magnus' daughter, Talon."

I looked at Charlie and knew her instantly. "Charlene?" I whispered. "My dad mentioned you in the letters he left for me. He loved you so much." So much I wondered if I'd ever find someone to love me like that.

Charlie's dark green eyes misted over, and she put a hand to her chest. "I love that old fool, too. He was stubborn and bossy, but the man had the biggest

MICK

heart of any man I ever came across." She surprised me with a tight hug. "It's nice to meet you, Talon. Once you get settled, come on back and I'll run you through everything."

My confusion must have shown on my face because Mick jumped in. "You own this place, along with the house and the land."

My eyes went round with surprise. I thought he'd left me a small café that sold sandwiches and chips, not all of this. "But what about Charlie? This has to be a mistake, he couldn't have left everything to me if he was the good man everyone says he was."

Charlie's warm hand fell to my shoulder. "You sure are a sweet one." She gently cupped one side of my face. "Don't worry, Magnus made sure to take care of me. That's just the kind of man he was."

"You sure?"

"Positive. I got my own house and a small plot of land. He gave it to me years ago, to make sure I was always taken care of."

Charlie's words finally broke the dam I'd erected around my heart and my emotions since finding Damon plowing into Abby on my kitchen table. I didn't cry after kicking him out, or when I sold everything in the apartment for two grand. I didn't cry as I packed up my little red SUV and said goodbye to Chicago. I wanted to cry because I'd been left all alone in the world sooner than I should have been. Wanted to cry for the man I never got to know. But somehow Charlie's softly spoken words were what made me crack. *Why, Mom?* I just wanted to know why she had lied to me my whole life. Why she'd taken that relationship from me, that love. I turned toward the wall when she walked off, using a napkin to dry my tears.

Finally under control, I took several long pulls from my beer as the busty Janine set our plates down. "Thanks."

She ignored me and kept her gaze trained on Mick, who acted like she wasn't even there. He raised his beer and said, "Don't be shy, sugar, dig in."

MICK

And in six words, Mick made me forget my grief as my body surged to life at that slow molasses drawl.

Yep, he was gonna be trouble with a capital T.

KB Winters

Chapter Two

Mick

The blistering heat of the day had finally relented as I left the clubhouse on the outskirts of Brently and headed toward Magnus' place. Now Talon's place, I thought with a smile. How my mind could be so full of such a tiny little thing, I didn't know. Maybe it had to do with our shared link to Magnus, but the petite raven-haired beauty had occupied my thoughts since she pulled up the dirt driveway four days ago.

Charlie had nothing but nice things to say about Talon who had decided to let the woman stay on to handle the business end of the diner while she took over the people and food end. She'd been in Black Betty every day making schedules, ordering inventory, and sitting down with the cook, Jimbo. She'd even managed to impress that old grouch which hardly anyone had been able to do.

Everywhere I went people talked about Talon. They wanted to know more about her, to tell me how sweet and kind she was. As if I didn't know already. She'd left me a thank you casserole and cookies at the diner, and she left it at that. She didn't leave her phone number or an invitation to her bed.

I was surprised but not put off in the least. As my bike came to stop outside her place, I knew it would come because she felt the tug, too. I set my helmet on the seat of my bike and climbed the steps, smiling at the Bob Seeger tunes floating through the windows. I rang the bell and waited, wondering how she'd react to seeing me on her doorstep.

"Mick," she said in a breathy voice that sent heat straight to my cock. "Come on in."

I groaned at the small blue dress she wore, adjusting the bulge between my legs when she turned

MICK

to reveal an expanse of bare back and legs. "Nice dress."

She gave me a saucy grin over her shoulder. "Want to borrow it?"

"Yeah. I'd like to use it to decorate my bedroom floor." I almost apologized until I heard the small gasp of surprise and saw the way she stumbled over her feet. Yeah, she felt it, too.

"I'll keep that in mind." She put a hand to her flushed cheeks. "What brings you by?"

Reluctantly I dragged my gaze from her toned legs and bare feet and looked into those big gray eyes shining with curiosity. "You. I thought you might like a tour of the area." *Why the fuck do I sound like a horny teenager with his first hard on around this woman?*

"On the bike?" I nodded, wondering if that was a deal breaker, though she seemed to enjoy it last time. "Can I wear this?"

Fuck yeah you can. "Please do." The thought of those bare legs wrapped around me had me imagining another scenario. I had to hold back the growl rumbling in my chest.

"Sure, I'd love that." She grabbed a small purse and slung it across her chest, stepped into a pair of canvas shoes and grabbed the helmet with a smile. "Ready."

Hell, I was more than ready to spend some time with Talon. She intrigued me, and that was something no woman had been able to do since I was a teenager. Back then girls were mysterious creatures to be won over, but the moment I joined the Navy the mystery was over. Fucking a SEAL had been more than enough, and even now, my cut was more than enough when I wanted to get laid. But something about Talon was different. She wanted me, but she was wary. "Hop on."

Her thighs squeezed mine and her arms wrapped around my waist, fingers linking just above my belt, and that sweet honeysuckle scent enveloped

MICK

me. I stopped at the mini-mart I owned along with the attached service station to grab a few things, and stuffed them in one of my saddlebags. The guys gave me shit about the bags, but with those bad boys loaded up, I could be ready to go at a moment's notice.

I rode through town even though she'd already seen all there was to see of interest in Brently, before taking one of the back roads that provided a view for miles. Small towns along the border illuminated the dark highway. Forty minutes later we circled back to a small crest that overlooked Brently and the border. "Oh," she gasped when I lifted her off the bike and held her close. I damn well wanted to feel her in my arms, but I also knew the long ride would make her legs wobbly. "Thanks."

Fuck me. That breathless whisper did things to me and Dick. "How are your legs?"

"They're vibrating," she laughed and held on to my forearms. "I guess that part takes some getting used to." Then she turned and gasped at the sight below. "Wow. This looks like an exhibit I saw once at an urban planning museum, how all the small towns look from above."

Urban planning museum? That husky laugh sounded again at the expression on my face.

"I always wondered who decided what a town would look like, and when the exhibit came to town I had to check it out."

When she asked about the view I told her. "That strip of concrete is the border that separates Brently from Tacapeo. It was easier during the mining days than having gunfights every other day, so together they built the strip."

"You love it here. I can hear it in your voice."

I supposed that was true. "This is the only real home I've ever had besides the military." I wasn't ready to tell her about bouncing around as a kid while my mom chased the next Prince Charming who turned out to be an asshole, so I pulled a blanket out

MICK

and laid it on the ground. Talon smoothed it out while I grabbed a couple beers from the other bag.

"Thanks. Cheers." She smiled and knocked her bottle against mine. "To starting over and new friends." Her gaze lingered on my mouth, and a pretty blush stole over her skin.

"Friends?"

She nodded. "I think friends is a good place to start."

Damn, she was frank. I fucking loved that shit. "Start what?"

Talon took a long sip and looked out over the small towns along the border and let silence settle between us. "You seem to be a hot commodity around here. You got a girlfriend, Mick?"

"No."

"A wife?"

"No."

"Friends with benefits?"

"Not lately." I set my beer down and turned to her, tangling my hand in her long black hair. "You?"

That lush mouth curved up at the corners, and I knew soon I'd learn exactly how that mouth tasted. "No wife or girlfriend to speak of."

"Talon," I groaned and brushed a thumb across her bottom lip, drawing a gasp from her.

Her tongue darted out, grazing the tip of my thumb. "Left behind my only family which consisted of a cheating ex and a skanky *former* best friend in Chicago."

I cupped her face, holding her in place until her eyes slammed into mine. Honesty, wariness, and a hint of vulnerability shone in those beautiful silver orbs. And desire, too. "So, no one to mind if I kiss you?" I shortened the distance between us, and her warm peppermint scented breath fanned over me.

"Just one who'll mind if you don't."

She shocked the hell out of me, following up those shyly spoken words with a bold kiss that stole

MICK

my breath. Full of passion and intensity, she tasted every inch of my mouth, licking my lips, and sucking my tongue until Dick stood up and wanted to play. She kissed like a wet dream, tugging her fingers through my hair to pull me closer. I pulled back. "Cherries," I growled.

"What?"

"I was wondering all night what you would taste like. The answer is cherries."

She must have liked that answer because she smiled and climbed on my lap, kissing me stupid while grinding against the hard cock nestled between her thighs.

Her small hands found their way under my shirt, gliding up my stomach to my chest. I groaned into her mouth when her nails scraped my nipples. "Talon."

She froze and pulled back just enough that we were eye to eye. "Too much?" Her nails did it again, drawing another groan from somewhere deeper in my gut. "I don't know what's happening to me, Mick. You make me crazy."

"Welcome to the club, darlin'."

Her response was to nibble my bottom lip while her hands wrapped around my body, nails gently raking down my back. Her hips continued to grind against me, and my control snapped. I held her hips down and dragged her back and forth across my cock until her body vibrated with desire. "Mick, please."

I flipped our positions and looked down into eyes nearly black with want. "Please?"

She nodded and grabbed my wrist, putting my hand inside the scrap of silk covering her pussy. "Please."

I sank one finger inside, groaning as her wet cunt clenched around me. "You're so tight, Talon, and wet. Are you wet for me?"

"Since you showed up on my doorstep," she panted.

MICK

While I finger fucked her, she undid my pants with one hand and reached inside to fist my cock. "Dick wants to play," I growled and pumped into her hand.

She laughed. "You named your cock Dick?"

"Yeah. He likes it."

"Dick seems happy to meet me," she said, still stroking my cock. "Maybe we should get a proper introduction?"

Fuck, this woman tore me up from the inside. On my knees, I let her free my cock completely, feeling Dick twitch under the heat of her gaze. She licked her lips and leaned closer, swiping her tongue over the tip. That was it, I needed to be inside her sweet, wet pussy. "As much I can't wait to fuck that pretty little mouth of yours, I need to be inside you."

"Oh, thank God," she said and licked my cock once more before I knelt between her thighs and plunged my cock inside her. "Mick. Now."

She was so goddamn wet I easily sank in to the hilt, groaning at how good she felt. She pulsed around me, flooding us both with her juices. "Talon."

"I'm good, you're just, ah, a little bigger than I'm used to."

"Fuck, you can't say that to a man and expect him not to respond."

Guileless gray eyes looked up at me. "I don't. I want you to respond, Mick. You make me fuckin' crazy."

I knew the feeling. I wanted her before, but now that I was buried deep inside her, I couldn't get enough. I pulled out and slammed in, letting the gasps and cries and moans urge me on. Fucking hard and fast, I slammed in and out while her hips moved in rhythm with mine, drawing us both closer to satisfaction. Lifting her ass so I could go deeper, I felt a light flash behind my eyes, the sensation unlike anything I'd ever felt while fucking.

MICK

"Mick, yes," she groaned and pinched her nipples. She opened her mouth, probably to tell me she was close, but I felt it. I felt every pulse of her pussy, every time her walls closed around me faster and faster. I knew she was on the edge. With a pinch of her clit I sent her soaring over. "Mick!" She screamed my name over and over as I plunged deeper and deeper, fucking her like my life depended on it.

In a way, it felt like it did. She still came as I fucked her, her juices dripping between us. Then I felt the tingling in my balls, the base of my spine, and moments later I roared my pleasure into the night. "Fuck, Talon."

She smiled up at me. A breathless whisper, "Mick," was all she said.

***

The sounds of the desert at night swirled around us, scorpions and snakes sang in the distance. Eyes closed so all my other senses were heightened, the sound of Talon's soft breathing and the musky scent of sex wafted over me. Calmed my racing heart and thoughts. I couldn't believe the intensity between us. It was unreal, unfathomable. Hell, I'd been with plenty of women, most of whom I'd never remember. But I already knew that for as long as I fucking drew a breath, I'd never forget the feel of her tight cunt squeezing around me. Coating me. Milking me.

She was a wildcat beneath that sweet Midwestern exterior, responsive and eager to please. My cock grew hard just reliving the moments of pleasure from earlier. I couldn't explain it, but something had passed between us in that moment when she squeezed my cock and shattered around me. I couldn't say what it was, but something Magnus said came back to me in that moment. *"Some men who live the way we do will fuck anything that moves, but men like you and me, we love hard and we love fast. And forever."* I thought he was full of shit back then, a man in love trying to get everybody else all loved up. Now I understood that shit completely.

MICK

Talon snuggled against me, one bare leg brushing against mine and one hand resting above my heart. I pulled her closer and kissed her neck, taking advantage of the closeness to grab one of those perky tits. "Lots of light for just two small towns," she said softly.

That drew my attention to the world around us. The Brently border didn't get a whole lot of traffic, especially this time of night when both towns rolled up the sidewalks. Hell, Black Betty, the two bars in town, and the CAOS clubhouse were the only places in town open past ten. But now I could see what she meant. An eighteen-wheeler came to a lurching stop on the Mexican side of the border, on the Brently side a half dozen bikes stopped about half a mile from the border.

I couldn't see shit from this distance, but I did recognize the flag on the bike in the rear. It was a flag I'd seen a lot. On the bike of Dagger, the Sergeant at Arms for CAOS. *What the fuck are they doing?*

Squinting, I couldn't see anything specifically, all I could tell was that something was going down, but that was more than enough for me. We didn't get our guns from the Mexicans, especially not after last year's ambush that killed Magnus, so it had to be something else. I knew it could only be one thing, and we didn't fucking deal in drugs so that couldn't be it. *Shit.* "You ready to head out?"

Talon nodded with a sleepy, satisfied smile. She quickly redressed, and I drove her back to her house, my mind still on the overlook at the border. "Can you tell me how my dad died?"

Shit. That was the last thing I wanted to talk about with my body still humming from the orgasms and my mind buzzing with what I'd just seen. Add to that I didn't have a whole lot of fucking answers for her, I'd rather take her back to bed. Instead, I nodded and accepted the beer she handed to me. "I wasn't there that night, but I know the cartel was pissed we'd burned a huge shipment of heroin coming over the border. We don't allow that shit in Brently and try to

MICK

keep it out of the goddamn state. They know it, but they tried and they failed. Magnus paid the price for it.

The tears in her eyes gutted me, and I pulled her into my lap, rubbing her back while she cried like a baby. "I just wish I could have met him once. Could have heard the sound of his voice. Hugged him just once." She snuggled closer, burying her face in the crook of my neck, and my body began to respond. "Can you stay with me tonight?"

Fuck yeah, I could. "If you want me to."

"I do," she answered softly and slid off my lap, staring down at me. Pulling the dress over her head, she tossed it at me and walked away. "I need you, Mick."

In a second, I was up on my feet and standing behind her, hands skimming up her legs, cupping her ass, and everywhere I could. "Where do you think you're going?" I pulled her back against me so she could feel how rock hard I was for her.

"To the bedroom," she moaned.

"Uh-uh, right here," I told her, ripping the sexy lace panties from her body and bending her over, sliding a finger in to test her readiness. She was more than ready. "So wet," I groaned, unfastening my belt and pants, shoving them down to free my cock.

"Please, Mick," she begged, sending another spear of lust right to my cock.

"Tell me, Talon." I spun her around and lifted her up, groaning when she wrapped those toned legs tight around my waist. "What do you want?"

"You." She grinned, gasping as I plunged into her. It wasn't a pretty fuck. It was hard and fast and rough. Up against the wall I pounded into her furiously until her pussy clenched me, drenched us both. "Mick!" The sound of my name on her lips as she came stripped the last of my control, and I let go. Moving toward my own orgasm as she continued to milk me dry.

MICK

"Let's go to bed, darlin'," I told her as I carried her a few feet to her room.

MICK

Chapter Three

Talon

I woke up snuggled against the hot, hard furnace that was Mick. He'd woken me up with a slow, languid fuck before he had to leave for work. I'd given him a long sensual kiss goodbye before going back to bed, and now my body ached so deliciously I could hardly pull myself from the bed. The sheets smelled of us, and when I inhaled the pillow Mick slept on, a smile crossed my face. That musky sexy scent that was all him slid up my nose and straight to my brain.

I had some serious issues if I was already swooning over this guy who I didn't really know much about. I knew he was hot and funny, and he fucked like a porn star. But I had no idea what his job actually was or what his motorcycle club did. Other than keeping cartel drugs out of Brently. Was that because they were good guys looking out for the community, or was it their attempt at squashing competition? I didn't know, and honestly, I couldn't think straight.

His sex had scrambled my brains, making it damn near impossible to make rational decisions. Add to that my feelings about losing my dad for a second time, and I felt more emotions than I knew what to do with. "And I thought leaving Damon and Abby was hard." These were real emotions far beyond those I battled with just months before.

And I had no fucking clue what to do with them.

On top of dealing with these emotions, I had plenty of other things to do like settle into my father's house. Or decide if I *would* settle into his house and turn it into my home. For the first time in my life I could do anything I wanted. I could sell the house, the land, the diner and head to places unknown to start

MICK

over. Figure out my own dreams for once. Or I could stay in Brently and make it my next chapter. With Mick.

"No. With me." I should have felt a bit crazy talking to myself while I dusted and cleaned out various desk drawers, but I had no one else to talk to. I couldn't make this decision with Mick as a factor. Not only had I just got out of a relationship, but I had gained a father, a home and a business. All those things needed my attention. Now.

In the bottom drawer of what used to be Magnus' desk I found legal papers and blueprints. I didn't know what to do with them, but I couldn't look away from the blueprints even though I had no idea how to read them. I spent an hour on them before getting dressed and heading to the diner. I now owned a freaking diner!

Luckily, things at the diner had been going well, thanks to Charlie who was the sweetest person around, and she had plenty of stories about my dad She knew a lot about running the diner, but she wasn't overbearing about my ideas. It felt nice to have someone to talk to, even if I didn't know her well enough to talk about all the thoughts going on in my mind.

"Hey, Talon." Charlie flashed a smile at me and nodded toward the back. "Go on and have a seat, I'll bring coffee and menus."

In the booth, I noticed Charlie already had some paperwork set up. Schedules and inventory sheets, invoices and all that stuff. For now, this would definitely be the start—at least—of my latest chapter. "Hey, Charlie, how's it going?"

She slid in the booth and gave an affectionate roll of her eyes. "The morning rush is over, and I'm glad about it."

I sipped my coffee while she showed me the ins and outs of running the diner. "Seems like a lot of work, but not more than I can handle."

"You'll do just fine, honey. Like you said, I'll take care of the managing everything. Just ask if you

MICK

want to know something. And you can handle the staffing, menus, and all that. We'll be good together. You'll see."

"You really don't feel like I'm coming in and displacing you, do you?"

"Not at all. Now I can take a day off once in a while."

Shit, I hadn't even thought of that. "If you need time off, just say the word."

She nodded and gave a wistful smile as she looked off in the distance. "You're like Magnus in that way. He was a rough man but sweet. Always thinking about others. He did what needed to be done for his club, but otherwise he was just a big ol' teddy bear." Sadness flashed in her eyes, but it was gone before I could be sure what I'd seen. "Never met a man like him who wasn't quick with his fists, but your dad was special. One of a kind, really." She gave me an assessing look. "You hanging around for a while?"

"Yeah." The answer hadn't been as clear just this morning, but it came out so easily, I knew it was the right choice.

"Good. I'm sure Mick will be real glad to hear it." Charlie's knowing smile unsettled me because it meant she saw something I wasn't ready for anyone to see.

"We just met."

"I've known Mick for five years, honey, and he's never taken an interest in any of the girls like he has with you. And believe me, they all want him and make no secret of it."

I'd seen that with my own eyes over the past week, but just in case I hadn't, Nadine trotted over for another reminder. And a glare for good measure. "Stay away from Mick. He's mine."

The venom in her voice surprised me, especially since Mick had said he'd never even touched her. "Just because you let the guys use you as a cum dumpster, Nadine, doesn't make any of

MICK

them yours." A brunette slid into the booth beside me with a saucy grin and a twinkle in her eye. "I'm Minx." She thrust a hand out, studying me a little *too* closely. "You have his eyes."

I blinked at the rapid change in conversation. "Me?"

"Yeah you." She bumped my shoulder. "Magnus had eyes like melted nickel, all deep and gray and broody. Made him look scary as hell, but damn, he was one of the good ones."

Charlie grinned and leaned in. "You're right. The hair was a dead giveaway, but combined with those eyes, wow." She snatched a napkin from the holder and dashed off.

Minx held a hand to stop my movement. "Don't worry about Charlie, she's a tough old broad. Loved Magnus with everything in her."

I didn't know how to respond. "I just wish I could have known him, for at least a day."

Minx nodded, thick chocolate waves tumbling around her shoulders and stopping just before her impressive cleavage that exploded from a sexy leather vest. "You would've loved him. I was terrified of him at first, thinking I'd been rescued from one hell just to be taken to another. But he saved me, really saved me. No strings other than I had to live a good life."

"How did he save you?"

"I'd been stolen from a park and put on a truck when I was thirteen. First, I ended up in a brothel house in Memphis and then New York, and I lost track after that. One day they put me in a truck with a bunch of others. For days we drove, and I'd been going through withdrawal because I'd been pumped full of drugs to keep me in line. That door opened and big ol' burly Magnus was there with an inch-deep scowl and a soft soothing voice." She shook her head and wiped away a tear. "He got CAOS to hire me as a bartender even though I was too young. I turned twenty-one two months before he died." Her hand smacked against the table. "Fuck! I hate crying."

MICK

"Me too," I told her, offering her a soothing hand. It was so strange to hear all these people who loved and missed a man I never knew.

"What are you up to now?" Minx didn't wait for an answer. "I'll give you a tour of the clubhouse." Before I could answer, she pulled me out of the booth and out into the sunny day.

***

They called it a clubhouse, but to me, it looked more like a compound. The last exit before the border lead right to a motel with an attached café. "That's owned by the club and a few girls work there, but one of the old-timers run it." Minx pointed to the various little buildings. "That outbuilding is basically a garage where they tinker with their bikes, though they don't call it that." She rolled her eyes and smiled.

"This is all CAOS property?"

"Yeah. They're not bad guys, but they do have diverse interests that I won't get into."

I half listened to her rattle off details as we got out of the car and entered a plain square structure made of brick and cement. Inside was dark, mahogany and black leather everywhere. The only hint of color was silver and gold studs that dotted leather chairs, sofas, stools and the like. On one side, a bar ran from the door to the back wall. The other side held several pool tables and dart boards. Further back, a bunch of young guys sat around a table, beer bottles littering the top as they laughed and shot the shit. "Wow this is something out of a movie.

Minx tossed her head back and laughed. "That about sums it up. Come on, let's get a drink and I'll introduce you to some of the guys."

I quietly followed her because there were too many guys here to make me feel comfortable, and some of them were very rough looking. Very. My head spun with introductions, and I knew I'd never remember all their names.

"Roddick here is the Prez, and that guy over there with the long greasy hair is Toro, the VP." I

MICK

smiled at Roddick but said nothing, he probably wondered who the hell I was and why I was there. "Dagger was here, but now he's gone. He's the Sergeant at Arms. That's Rocky and Wagman, the Road Captain and the Secretary."

"Nice to meet you." I practically stammered, but these guys were huge and kind of scary. Not like Mick who was huge and…yummy.

"And finally, four eyes over there is Baz, the Tech Captain and the bulging biceps is Torch, the enforcer. They're all nice as shit, some of the time."

"Who knew Magnus had such a smoking hot daughter?" I was pretty sure that came from Wagman.

I froze as arms wrapped around me. "You look like someone dropped you off in the wild." Mick's deep voice vibrated in my chest, and I couldn't suppress the shiver that went down my spine.

I laughed and leaned into him. "It feels like it. I thought these places were just made up for TV, but

55

holy shit, this is all real!" The guys around me erupted in laughter, and a few of the guys stepped forward to share stories of my dad. Some didn't, but I didn't think much of it, maybe they weren't close to him. Despite the tattoos, leather, and giant rings, Mick's friends seemed nice.

"I'm glad you stopped by." He pressed a gentle but forceful kiss against my mouth. "I hated leaving you this morning."

"But you left me so happy," I murmured against his lips before Minx pulled me away.

"You can kissy face later. Let's finish the tour." She stopped in front of oversized double doors with the CAOS symbol carved in it, one half on each door. "This is Church and no one other than the guys are allowed inside. Down this hall are rooms for prospects and any club members who need a place to crash."

I peeked in the open door and a man with a scruffy blond beard stared at me while a woman was on her knees giving him a blow job. I couldn't look

MICK

away, but I didn't want to look. "That the real reason for these rooms?" I wondered if Mick and I became something, would I have to worry about this?

"That happens a lot. Plenty of the girls here will fuck whoever will have them in hopes one of them will turn 'em into an ol' lady."

"Are you an old lady? What's an old lady?"

"Hell no. I'm just an employee." Her words said that, but the lingering look she shot at the hot blond talking to Mick said otherwise. He waved us over, and with a groan Minx pulled me forward.

"Talon this is Cash, we served together. Everyone calls him CJ."

"Thanks for your service, Cash. Pretty cool name, too." He smiled and took my hand, revealing bright green eyes and dimples.

"Says the chick named Talon," he joked. "Your old man was solid. I knew him only for a little while, but his presence is missed around here."

I didn't know what to say, though I appreciated the sentiment. "Thanks."

"You ready to get out of here?" Mick was already pulling me away before I could answer him or say goodbye to Minx.

"My car is at the diner."

"I'll give you a ride to your car, and you can owe me one later," he growled and nipped at my ear. Mick slid his helmet over my head, kissing me hard as he fastened the chin strap. I knew I was in trouble this morning, but now I knew without a doubt I was in deep fucking trouble with this guy.

MICK

Chapter Four

Mick

As reluctant as I felt to leave Talon, I had spent all day in bed with her, and there was something else occupying my mind other than the sexy raven-haired beauty. The shit I saw my first night with Talon on the overlook just wouldn't go away. The club—*my* club—was involved in some shady shit. and I wanted to know what. Hell, I needed to know.

No one had said anything about a recent score, and there certainly hadn't been any money sent my way like usual. We got a score and split the proceeds. Every damn time. That was how it went. The fact that more than a week had gone by with nothing told me everything I needed to know. CAOS—at least some of the guys—were nowhere near as lily white as they pretended to be.

So I got up and gave Talon two orgasms in the shower before hopping on my bike to meet Cash at the overlook. Just the idea of that place now gave me a silly ass grin.

"What, or should I say who put that smile on your face?"

"Nothing. Have you noticed anything weird around here lately?" Cash had only been patched for about a year, so he knew the inner workings of the club, though not as well as I did.

"You mean like a few guys more flush than the rest?" Cash saw more than anyone gave him credit for. It had made him an asset in the military and now it would, too.

But fuck, if he noticed, I wondered if anyone else had. "Yeah." I noticed at the clubhouse a few days ago, and I wanted to believe it was just that I didn't know them all that well so they were easy to suspect.

MICK

CAOS was like any other organization with small cliques within it. Roddick, the Prez, was a cool guy, but I was hard pressed to believe any of this shit could go down without his say so. The penalty was too severe to act without the approval of the club. That shit was sewn into the bylaws.

"What are you thinking?"

I blew out a breath trying to decide how much I wanted to share with Cash. I trusted him with my life because he'd earned it, but I wasn't sure if I should lay this shit on his shoulders yet. But I had to tell someone to see if I was losing my mind or if there was trouble. "I was here with Talon recently and saw a deal go down. I'm pretty sure one of the bikes belonged to Dagger."

"Shit!" He kicked at the ground in restless frustration that I understood. "What are we gonna do, man?"

I grinned and pulled at my beard. Once a SEAL always a fucking SEAL. I was glad Cash was willing to dig into this with me, knowing the risks. "We're gonna find out what the fuck is going on, who we can trust and then, brother, we're gonna fucking take care of it. Just like old times."

Cash grinned that schoolboy smile of his that caused a lot of shit in the navy. "Fuck yeah. I'll see what I can find out." He stared out into the dark desert night, seemingly lost in thought. "You think this shit has anything to do with Magnus' death?"

I frowned and turned to Cash. "What do you mean?"

"Seriously?" He sighed and shook his head. "There was supposedly this big ass shootout with the Mexicans, and no one was even injured but the best shooter in the club—Mag—and he's the only fucker who took a bullet? I ain't buying that even with someone else's money." His final look said, *Are you?*

"Shit, me either. I didn't think anyone else had doubts." As refreshing as it felt to hear I wasn't alone in my suspicions, all I wanted to do was crawl back into bed with the ebony-haired vixen who had me under her spell.

MICK

***

"Don't tell the hot little owner of Black Betty, but I went over to Creston to get some Chinese takeout." I held up a white bag with some Asian characters on the front and smiled when Talon opened the door.

She crossed her arms over her chest and kicked her hip to the side, sending me a saucy grin. "I'm sure you can work something out with her."

She turned and walked away, and my jaw clenched at the sight of her ass in a pair of tight pink shorts that hugged her cheeks and offered up a glimpse of shadow just below. And fuck, she wasn't wearing a bra in that loose-fitting tee. "Name your price." In that outfit with her girl next door grin, I would give her whatever the fuck she wanted.

She blushed and took the bag from me, setting the cartons on the patio table. "Thanks for bringing dinner. I really didn't feel like cooking tonight." She went back for plates, silverware, and beers, and I knew in that moment I could love her. Just like that.

"Then maybe you owe me." I winked at her, taking full pleasure in the shiver she couldn't hide if she wanted to. Laughing, she muttered something about me being incorrigible and pointed a half-eaten eggroll in my direction. "I need to talk to you about something, babe."

She froze but quickly recovered. "Sounds ominous."

I knew what she was thinking, but now was not the time to tell her just how wrong she was. That talk would come later. After I figured this club shit out. "We're solid, babe. This is about Magnus."

Swallowing her eggroll, she took a long pull from her beer and looked at me. "Okay, hit me with it."

I couldn't help but smile at her resilience. She looked like a delicate rose petal, soft and fragile, but she wasn't. After what her asshole ex and her so-called best friend had done, despite being denied a lifetime with her father, she was still bright and sunny and ready to face life head on. *She was fucking*

MICK

perfect. "I don't know how to say this, so I'm just gonna say it. I'm not sure your father's death was what it appeared." By the time I explained my suspicions, all the color had drained from her already pale face.

"You think your club was involved?"

I gave a short nod. "I think what I know so far leans that way. But until I get things figured out, you can't get involved in this. Don't try to investigate on your own, and don't go asking questions. I mean it. Please."

The look she gave me was part trust and part defiance. Her eyes never left mine as she weighed her options, coming to a decision minutes later. "Okay, I won't say anything. But please don't keep me in the dark. I promise to be safe and smart and not at all one of those armchair detective women. As long as I know what's happening and what you find out." She looked deep into my eyes as though she could make me understand how important it was that she could trust me, so I decided to make it easy on her.

"You can trust me. I want you safe, and I promise you I will find out what happened."

She stood and straddled my hips, wrapping her arms around my neck so we were eye to eye again. "I trust you. I don't know about the guys in your club, but I feel like I know you. Don't make me regret it, yeah?"

Damn, I really could love this woman. "I promise the only thing you'll regret is not taking advantage of this hard on and those little shorts."

She snorted a laugh and covered her face in embarrassment. "Is one eggroll enough fuel for all that?"

"Only one way to find out, darlin'."

MICK

Chapter Five

Talon

I finally got a chance to sit down with the books for Black Betty, and what I found left me a little confused. I had some management experience but mostly in retail, so I figured the basics were pretty much the same. I couldn't have been more wrong. The bills from the past year were higher than they should've been, and I had to figure it out.

I didn't want to blame anyone, particularly Charlie, but I needed to know if someone was stealing from me or my father. I spent the better part of the morning and afternoon going through orders for the past two years and creating a spreadsheet of expenses and profit. The first thing I noticed was that the produce bill had doubled six months before Dad's death, but the amount of produce ordered and delivered had not. *Weird.*

I promised Mick I wouldn't investigate and I wouldn't, but I saved it all to a flash drive to show him later.

"Everything all right?" Charlie smiled down at me, a cup of coffee in one hand and pie in the other.

"Yep. Just checking past orders so I know what a good month looks like compared to a bad month." I was curious if Charlie was involved in any of this? It seemed clear to me she loved my dad, but money did strange things to people. The diner and the house plus the land it sat on would have gone to her if not for me, and I had to wonder if she even knew about me before Mick found me. I physically shook that thought off because it felt too scary. Too real to think about.

"If you have any questions just let me know," she said so casually I figured I must be wrong about it. Still, it wouldn't hurt to be more diligent.

MICK

I nodded and finished placing the new orders before backing up everything on a new flash drive. A quick glance at the clock told me I'd been here long enough, and the tension in my stomach said the time had come for me to go home. *Home.* Never thought I'd actually call this place home.

"Hey, girl, what's up?" Minx breezed in as she always did, wearing a blinding smile and her cleavage on display. Today she wore a denim dress that hit mid-thigh and red and white cowboy boots that were adorable and sexy.

"Not much, just finishing up some orders and going over the books. What's up with you?"

"Just thought I'd pop in and see if you wanted to hang."

I liked Minx. She seemed genuine and not quite as hard as some of the women I'd met so far. "Sure, what'd you have in mind?" She pulled me up from the chair, and I grabbed the stuff I wanted to take with me. After stuffing it all in my car, I grabbed my sunglasses and looked at her. "Where to?"

"Let's enjoy one of the real pleasures of small town living. A nice leisurely walk." She flashed a grin, lowering her cowboy hat on her head to shield her from the sun.

We walked along First Street which was Brently's answer to Main Street. All the shops had colorful awnings with cute old timey names. The sidewalks were made up of wooden slats giving it that old west feel from the movies. "This is nice," I told her, enjoying the way everyone had a ready smile and a kind greeting.

"Yeah, it's a great place to live about ninety percent of the time. When things get scary it sucks, but we all know CAOS will take care of us."

She spoke with such authority, but I wondered if maybe CAOS was responsible for the ten percent that sucked.

"Oh, let's go into Two Scoops." She explained that Trudy owned and ran the ice cream shop in addition to making many of her own flavors. "She's Dagger's ol' lady."

MICK

"I'll be right with you," a husky voice called out from somewhere in the back. The shop was decorated in sea green and carnation pink everywhere. The logo, the gingham tablecloths, the checkered wallpaper border. It all felt welcoming and fun.

"It's just me, Trudy, and I've brought our newest resident to test out your creations."

Trudy entered with a hesitant smile, but she greeted me with kindness. "Nice to meet you, Talon."

"You, too. This is a great shop, I love the soda shoppe décor."

Her face brightened at the compliment. "Thank you. Everyone laughs about it, but I'm glad to see someone appreciates it." Her smile fell quickly, and worry created tension lines around her eyes. "Have you guys heard anything about the ride last night?"

I looked to Minx because she would know more than I would. "I haven't heard about it, but I know Mick was with me last night."

Minx's eyes lit up at my admission, but she wrapped an arm around Trudy. "Sorry, hon, I know nothing of a ride last night."

I didn't know Trudy at all, but I could recognize the distress written all over her. I'd seen my mother distraught enough over a man to know the signs. "Dagger didn't come home last night, and he wasn't at the clubhouse."

Minx held her tight, soothing her with soft noises before pulling back. "I'm sure he's fine. We're on our way there anyway, so I'll see what I can find out for you, 'kay?" Trudy sniffled and grabbed a napkin, nodding her agreement. "Great, now let's show off some of your fancy ice cream skills for the new girl."

I smiled at the way Minx put everyone around her at ease. I was sure her background had something to do with her skills at diffusing situations, but still I envied it. After tasting a few spoons of Trudy's amazing creations, I knew this place would become my favorite snack shop, and unlike Chicago, I could

MICK

eat here all year long. "They're all so amazing, but I'm going with the peanut butter mousse and mint chocolate chip."

"That's a pregnancy mix if I ever heard of one," Minx groaned and took her toffee and coffee ice cream with a grin.

"You have no idea. I used to mix peanut butter with the mint chocolate chip as a kid, but thanks to Trudy I don't have to do that anymore. Delicious stuff." I grinned, hoping my compliment did something to ease her worry.

Back out under the scorching midday sun, we walked and ate mostly in silence, but Trudy's worry really struck me. Part of it had to do with my conversation with Mick, but the other part was…I didn't know. She seemed like a strong, capable woman. She and Dagger had a couple kids, and she knew this life. If she was worried, she probably had reason to be. "What do you think that's about?" I asked Minx, nodding my head toward Two Scoops.

She shrugged, but the light within her dimmed just a smidge. "I don't really bother myself with club business unless I need to. Otherwise, the guys tell me what I need to know."

I knew I couldn't lead a life of blind loyalty like that, but I understood why she did. They had literally saved her life, and that was how she'd chosen to repay them. "Right, but do you think something is up? I'm pretty sure there was no ride last night."

Minx stopped and studied me for a minute under the brim of her hat before she started walking again. "Apparently, I'm not the only one who does." She gave me a pointed look. "I don't know for sure, and if I want to live to see twenty-two then I can't go digging around. Got it?"

I nodded because I got it. More than she knew.

"Good, let's head to the clubhouse."

My stomach felt uneasy, and the ice cream turned to lead in my gut. But we headed back to my car anyway.

MICK

***

Going to the clubhouse left me feeling even more tense than my first visit. This time I knew what to expect, but that didn't stop the roiling in my belly, the feeling I shouldn't be there. As soon as we walked through the large double doors I spotted Mick, looking like a walking, talking wet dream in jeans that scandalously cupped his thighs and ass and the black leather of his cut hanging deliciously from his broad shoulders. And just like that, all the tension drained from my body and a new kind settled like lava in my veins. He was deep in conversation with Cash, so all I got was a flash of his come hither grin.

"Let's mingle. He'll find you when he's done." Minx pulled me to the bar where a young prospect with movie star looks stood behind it flashing a dimpled smile.

"What can I get you, ladies?"

"None for me, thanks. I have work to do still." I stood around with Minx, chatting with a few of the guys and some of the women who always seemed to be around.

"Hear that, Miss High and Mighty is too good to drink with us," a woman with black hair and blonde streaks sneered in my direction. I glared at her until she turned away because I refused to let anyone disrespect me ever again. Besides, I'd be jealous that Mick was sharing my bed if I were them. I smiled and laughed at the right times, but something about being at the clubhouse didn't seem right. Maybe it was because one or more of the girls might have wanted Mick and I had him—or because someone had a hand in my dad's death.

I leaned over the bar where the handsome prospect stood, ready to mix. "Can you tell me how to make a Mai Tai?" I could have looked it up online, but I figured asking him would give me a few minutes' reprieve from chatting with anyone else. He showed me how to make it with that ever-present grin, but I felt a prickle of unease shoot down my spine just moments before we were interrupted.

MICK

"You know, Mick isn't the only club member around. I might like a ride, too." Toro laughed when I shook off his touch. "Mick can't keep you all to himself," he growled, trailing a finger down my jaw.

I smacked his hand away. "Too bad no one has a say in what I do but me." The guy was gross and made my protective instincts kick in big time.

"I'll be seein' you soon, Talon."

"Not if I can help it," I grumbled and looked around the room with an assessing gaze. Guys like Toro and the snarky little bitch was the reason I began to wonder if hanging around here, around these men and this life that had gotten my father killed, was the smartest thing for me.

"Everything okay?" Mick asked as he wrapped his arms around me, his deep voice in my ear drawing a shiver from me.

I wanted to stay right there, enveloped in his scent. His strong tattooed arms. But I couldn't. "That guy gives me the creeps. Wanted me to know he was up for a ride. On me." I couldn't help but notice Mick was preoccupied with something else, at least I hoped so. If not then I'd read things between us badly. Last week he'd shown his jealous side when a cashier flirted with me at the grocery store, but now he had nothing to say. Weird.

"Yeah look, babe, I've got some shit to take care of around here, and I probably won't stop by tonight." He pressed a kiss to my cheek, but he didn't even look at me. "Call and let me know you made it home all right, yeah?"

"Sure," I answered absently and went in search of Minx. I'd been ready to go the moment we stepped into the clubhouse, but now I just wanted to get home. Minx and Cash were in a heated discussion by the door. Perfect. "Hey, Minx, what are you up to tonight? Want to come over?" I didn't need Mick to have a good time, and I needed to make my own friends so that when this ended I wouldn't feel compelled to leave town.

"Yeah. I'll meet you there in thirty?"

MICK

"Make it an hour, I need to stop for some supplies." Which mostly meant I needed booze, but I also needed food and snacks.

***

"I figured it was rude to show up empty handed. Not that I know that, mind you, but I heard it on a show once." Minx walked in and put down a Black Betty bag with two chicken dinners and a case of beer. "I haven't had a girls' night in forever. All the chicks here are ol' ladies who are crazy jealous or old as shit, and the young ones are looking to become ol' ladies." She held up a beautiful multi-colored glass pipe. "I figured we could use some Lemon Haze to get the night started." She wiggled her perfectly shaped brows.

"Is that pot?" She nodded, and I was intrigued. I'd never smoked pot before, but I knew they gave it to my mom while she was in cancer treatment. And I did have a mild curiosity about it. "Okay, let's give it a shot."

"Yay," she squealed with too much glee. "I'm corrupting you!"

I didn't think that was true, but it made her feel good to think it. After a few puffs, I didn't feel all that stressed any longer. We talked and shared stories about growing up, and Minx told me all about life in Brently. Most of it amused me—could have been the pot—some of it left me wary.

Listening to her stories had me shaking with laughter. "Everyone is a little rougher than usual, but most of 'em are good people just trying to make a life for themselves."

I believed that but decided to keep my feelings on the CAOS clubhouse to myself. "So, tell me about you and Cash."

Her face turned an amusing shade of pink that told me my hunch was right. "Nothing to tell. He's a Boy Scout, and I've already been saved as much as I can be."

"He's hot, though, and he seems nice."

MICK

"Oh, he's both of those things in spades. Just not for me."

I had a feeling Minx was fooling herself, but I didn't know her well enough to say it, so I just nodded and popped open another beer. We'd drank a lot. I felt it when my legs went wobbly on the way to the kitchen to pick up the dinners from Black Betty. And then again when my vision went hazy around the edges.

Hours later, Minx had already passed out on one end of the sofa, and I was nodding off myself. The last time I looked at the clock it was three in the morning. Mick hadn't even bothered to call.

It was a good reminder for me. This relationship, although new and exciting, probably wouldn't be my last. And I needed to remember that.

Chapter Six

Mick

"Are you sure they said there was a meet tonight?" Cash sat impatiently in the passenger seat of one of the old loaner trucks I kept at the service station. "We've been out here forever, and you brought some seriously shitty snacks."

"I heard Toro telling one of the pass-arounds that he and some of the guys had a meeting tonight but that she should be waiting for him when he returned to the clubhouse." I'd overheard the conversation after Talon left the house a few days ago. I'd been about to tear into him for disrespecting my woman when I heard it.

"And you read that to mean...shit, do you hear that?" The familiar rumble of choppers sounded in the distance. "Hand me those binoculars."

"Hell no," I grunted and picked them up for myself. "These are for experts."

Cash barked out a laugh. "I have eyes too, asshole. What do you see?"

"Four bikes, definitely CAOS. Dagger's not there this time. Roddick either." That part relieved me because I actually thought of the man as a friend, but the whole goddamn thing pissed me off because it meant they were going against the club. "They're just hanging out now about a half mile from the border."

Cash absorbed my words, but he seemed distracted. "We'll figure it out, man, that's why we're here. What's up with you and Talon?"

That was the question of the hour, wasn't it? "I don't know. I like her, a lot more than I've ever liked a woman. I think she might be it for me."

MICK

"But?" Cash prompted with a smug smile and a roll of his hand to urge me on.

"But I pulled back this week, and she followed my lead. I needed to focus on fixing this shit before I could focus on us. I haven't seen her or spoken to her since she showed up at the clubhouse last week. What's up with you and Minx?"

"Nothing worth mentioning. The woman's pricklier than a fucking cactus." He let out a pitiful laugh, but I noticed movement and pulled the binoculars back up. "You just need to grovel, maybe buy her something that means something."

"A dark SUV just pulled up across the border, and the bikes are on the move." Cash had dug out the cheap pair of binoculars I had in the glove box and aimed them at the border. We both watched in silence as five men stepped out of the SUV.

"Shit, that's Lazarus Ocatella of the Mexican Devils."

"Those fuckers deal in pussy, coke, and weed. We don't need more girls, so unless bullets start flying in the next minute, we have our answer." Cash's words were cold, efficient, like the solider he'd been for more than a decade. "I'm gonna get this shit on video."

We both watched through the barrier of lenses as Toro took a leather bag that could only contain money and shook hands with Lazarus. "Un-fucking-believable!"

Everyone returned to their vehicles and the SUV crossed over the border, following the bikes down the road. I started the engine to follow at a distance. This time of night there wasn't much traffic in Brently or the main highway so I needed to stay back, but thanks to Toro's chopper it wouldn't be hard to keep them close. "Fuck!" I smacked the steering wheel as the truth of the situation became clear. "They're giving those assholes protection, and I'm sure you can guess why." We didn't need to guess, though, because we followed them a few more miles

MICK

up the road and the SVU made a turn while the bikes continued ahead, presumably back to the clubhouse.

"Take the dirt road."

I cut the lights and followed the SUV while Cash kept filming as they bounced down the dirt road. Lazarus stepped out and walked around the back of the truck where he pulled a brick from the back and handed it another man, one I didn't recognize. "Definitely coke or heroin, maybe both."

"Yeah, and that's not all. Toro, Rocky, Wags and one of the fucking prospects helped get this shit over the border."

That meant we needed to figure out who we could trust before we could come up with a fucking plan. "Let's get home."

***

After dropping Cash off at the clubhouse, I took my bike and headed to Talon's place where I stood on her porch for several long minutes while I worked out what to say to her. She'd likely be pissed off, and I had very little experience with pissed off females these days. The women around here didn't get all that upset, especially at a patched member, and a quick flash of my green eyes usually did the trick.

That wouldn't happen here.

The door opened. "You gonna stay out there all night or be a man and come in?"

Ouch. Well I guess I had my answer. "I was just getting up my courage." I flashed a smile, but her lips remained in a straight line as she waved me in.

"Well I guess you can do it inside as well as out. Right?"

"Yeah," I sighed and walked in, but I couldn't deal with this tension between us so I stopped and turned to her, cupping her face. "Yell at me later, but right now I need this." My mouth slammed into hers, devouring her in my desperate need to taste her. To be closer to her. To *feel* her. I kissed her long and hard until we were both breathless and my cock strained

MICK

against my zipper, so desperate to bury myself deep in her. "That's better," I growled.

"That was nice, but not exactly what I was expecting since I haven't heard from you all week."

There was no heat behind her words, but I could tell her feelings were hurt and she wasn't pleased with me. "I know, babe. I'm an asshole and I'll explain everything, but first I need a shower."

She pushed me back, but I saw the way her lips curled as she walked past. "Don't expect me to wash your back."

I had to laugh at her words because Talon was a woman you couldn't keep down. She might be mad but she still responded to my kisses, and she was damn happy to see me.

She disappeared into the kitchen and I went to her room, undressing and taking the world's fastest shower because I wanted to settle things between us. Seven minutes later, I had a towel wrapped around my waist as I strolled into the kitchen.

"I figured you might be hungry," she said and pushed a thick slice of lasagna across the table. "Don't get too excited, it's vegetarian because I wasn't expecting you." She grabbed two beers and slid one my way. "Eat and then you can tell me why you're avoiding me until now. At midnight."

Yeah, I knew exactly what she meant. She thought I stopped by to fuck her when I'd avoided her all week. Because I'm an asshole. "Cash and I did some recon tonight to see what we could find out. It wasn't good, darlin'." I told her everything because she swore she could handle it, and I believed her. "I shouldn't have disappeared on you like that and I'm fucking sorry, but I needed to get to the bottom of this." Shit, I knew I couldn't explain it, but I did my best. "I have to ride with these guys, sometimes across states and count on them to have my back in case any shit goes down. I have to be able to trust them."

"I get that. But what does that have to do with a couple phone calls or text messages? For all I know

MICK

you weren't figuring shit out, you were with one of your *pass-arounds*."

I scoffed, "I definitely wasn't doing that. Look, baby, I'm sorry but I'm not your ex. I'm trying to figure out if my club had anything to do with killing the man who was like a father to me."

"Thank you for that," she answered primly and stood to rinse her bottle and dump it in the recycling bin she kept on the back porch. "Good luck."

Good luck? That sounded like goodbye to my ears, and I couldn't have that. "That's all you have to say?"

"What else do you want me to say, Mick? I accept your explanation, but maybe we should just stop this until you find what you're looking for. I wouldn't want to be a distraction."

Her words were right but they sounded off, like she didn't mean them. "No."

"What do you mean, no?"

I went over to her, one hand on the knot keeping the towel around my waist. "I mean we're not stopping anything. You're mine, and I'm yours."

"I thought so, too." She took a step back and raked a hand through her thick black waves. "But I've been wrong before."

"Goddammit, Talon, you're mine. Don't fucking fight it," I growled, pinning her against the sliding glass door with my body, nipping her ear. "You don't want to fight it, babe, and I'm so damn tired of fighting."

"Yeah, you just want to fuck, don't you, baby?" she shot back, but I heard the breathy quality of her voice. She was as turned on as I was.

"You want to fuck, too. You want me to fuck you and then you want to hop on my cock and fuck me. Don't you?"

"No."

"Liar." I pressed my cock between her legs, and the deep moan that she released told me she was

MICK

still here. With me. "Tell me, Talon." I licked across her neck, biting down and soothing it with more kisses. "Tell me."

"Yes, Mick, I want you to fuck me. And then I want to ride your cock until I come all over you."

That's all I needed to hear. Without a word, I grabbed the little scrap of silk she wore under that flowery dress and yanked until the fabric tore.

"No." She pushed at my chest until I fell back against the counter, and then dropped to her knees. I groaned, and she smiled up at me while her hands made quick work of the towel until my cock sprang free. "Such a beautiful cock," she purred and took me deep in her hot, wet mouth.

Jaysus! She felt so good around my cock, and I couldn't stop my hips from thrusting forward, sliding deeper down her throat. "Yeah, baby. You want me to fuck that pretty little mouth of yours?" She nodded, speaking around my cock, and sending vibrations through my balls. I growled and pumped harder when she grabbed my ass, sinking her nails into my cheeks. "You like it," I told her.

Silver eyes widened in excitement when I began to fuck her mouth, grabbing her hair and twisting it around my fist. I'd never been so fucking turned on in my life, but I needed her pussy and pulled out with a pop that made my nuts tingle.

"Mmm, that made me so wet," she purred.

"You're trying to kill me," I told her as I lifted her up, kissing her hard enough that I knew she'd have beard burn tomorrow. "I'm gonna eat that sweet cunt of yours, but first I need to be inside you."

"Yes," she moaned as I slipped a finger into her tight, hot cunt. She was more than ready for me. She was begging for me. "Now, baby. Fuck me…"

She jumped in my arms, wrapping her legs around my waist, and I fucked her hard and fast up against the stainless-steel fridge. Long and hard and deep, I pounded into her because I loved the way her pussy dripped and clenched when I went deep. I hit

MICK

that spot that made her eyes close, and she made that dirty growl in the back of her throat. "I can't get enough."

"Harder."

I gave her exactly what she wanted, what she needed. Shoving my cock deep until those telltale pulses squeezed me tight, and she shouted my name on a keening cry that had my spine stiffening and my come shooting deep inside her until she was full. Of me. "Oh, babe."

A nervous laugh erupted from her, shaking us both along with the bottles on top of the fridge. "That was perfect." She smacked a kiss against my neck and slid down my body until we separated. "I'll be back."

We both cleaned up and put some clothes on before meeting again in the kitchen. I grabbed us a couple beers and opened the old-school cookie jar on the counter, smiling when I pulled out peanut butter chocolate chip. My favorite. "You made cookies."

"Yeah well having sex with myself doesn't really take up a lot of time, so," she trailed off and took a long pull from her beer. "Have a seat. We need to talk."

"The worst four words in the English language," I grumbled. "Are you leaving?"

"No. I'm not, but I found a few things I think you should know about." Her eyes darkened to melted gun metal, a contemplative expression on her beautiful face. Raven hair mussed from my hands.

"You've been digging?"

"No, but this might go faster if you stop guessing and just let me tell you." Her lips twitched at the corners, and I nodded for her to continue. "I think something fishy was—or *is*—going on with the produce delivery at the diner. I didn't investigate because I promised I wouldn't, but I do have it for you to see it because it is my place now." She grabbed her laptop from the coffee table and brought it to me, inserting a flash drive and stepping back for me to look.

MICK

I started going through the spreadsheets she created for each month of the past four years, and I could see very clearly what she meant. Fruits and vegetables from Mexico, but more importantly the consistency of the orders seemed off. "Magnus would have never ordered produce from Mexico if he could help it, even with us being so close to the border. Always preached about buying American and saving jobs and shit."

"Do you think this could be helpful to you?"

"Yeah, I do." I didn't have all the pieces put together yet, so I didn't want to bother her with theories or get her hopes up. "Just be careful with anyone who isn't me or Cash, yeah?"

Damn, this girl seemed just perfect as she climbed on my lap, straddling my hips so we were face to face, my cock nestled between her thighs exactly where it should be. "There's something else. The day I went to the clubhouse, Minx and I stopped at Two Scoops, and Trudy was pretty worried because

Dagger hadn't come home. *Still* hasn't come home. Do you think he's involved or…?"

A big fat fucking *or*. I didn't think Dagger was involved, at least not on purpose, and his disappearance had me more worried than ever. "Shit. You didn't say anything, did you?"

She play slapped my cheek. "I told you I wouldn't. Don't you trust *me*?"

"I do, or I wouldn't tell you any of this. And thank you for telling me," I stood and carried her to the bedroom, kissing her again. "And thank you for not doing anything else."

Her smile punched me in the gut and I was reminded again, this girl was *it* for me. "I told you I wouldn't." Leaning back on the bed, robe gaping open at the thigh, she looked like a fucking goddess.

She leaned back on the bed, looking good enough to eat. "I want to still be mad at you, Mick, but I think I'm in love with you."

MICK

I leaned over and fixed my mouth to hers, pouring everything I felt into that kiss while my hands made their way between her legs. She was still wet or maybe wet again for me, and I rubbed my calloused fingers against her clit, swallowing her moans. In less than a minute, her thighs tightened around my fingers and she cried out my name.

Satisfied with the pink flush of her skin, I slowly removed my fingers and brought them up to my mouth, licking them clean. "When you're sure, let me know." I stood up, gave her one last kiss, and walked out.

MICK

Chapter Seven

Talon

"Thanks, Charlie. I'm glad you agree with me." I'd straightened my spine this morning and hoisted up my big girl panties so I could finally talk to Charlie about the produce supplier. Technically, it couldn't be considered getting involved because the diner was my business, and I had a right to make changes. Plus, her ready agreement meant Charlie had no role in my father's death.

"No problem, honey. I never understood why Magnus changed it anyway." She cradled one side of my face, something she did often, and it made me feel cared for. Nurtured.

I wrapped my arms around her, feeling her grief must be unimaginable. "I'm sorry for your loss, Charlie."

"Me too, honey, I wish he could have seen you. He'd be so tickled you're here." I loved hearing that, but every time I did it made me angry with Mom, and since I couldn't be angry with a dead woman, those feelings felt pointless.

Waving Charlie off, I said my goodbyes and made my way home. I desperately needed a shower after making the girls give the kitchen a thorough scrub. Most of them didn't even like me, so it was no problem being a hard ass if it meant getting things done.

The short drive home gave me time to pull my thoughts together as I watched the fiery sun come closer and closer to kissing the horizon. The sun's movements were purposeful, automatic whereas mine felt…haphazard. I looked around, seeing everything my dad had built with his life. A motorcycle club that boasted a massive clubhouse as

MICK

well as more than a dozen businesses, a long-term relationship with a good woman and many lifelong friendships.

What did I have to show? Not a goddamned thing. Everything I had now—the house, the business, the land, even Mick—was all thanks to him. Maybe I was being melodramatic, or maybe rereading the letter he'd left me had taken my mind to places it shouldn't go. I decided to let Charlie's words stand as the truth. Magnus loved Mick, and I'd like to think he'd love the fact that we're together thanks to him. I think he'd be happy that I switched produce suppliers, unless of course that decision brought hell and thunder to my front door.

I pushed through the front door and reminded myself that negative thoughts like that didn't help anything. No matter what Mick found—and I had no doubt he would find his answers—things would play out the way they were meant to in the end. Good or bad.

After a quick shower, I shoved all thoughts of Mick aside because I needed to get my libido in check, and thinking about him had a way of making me think of orgasms, which in turn made me *want* orgasms. But I needed to get dinner started because this was part of the new and improved Talon, making healthy dinners at night like a grownup. So, I moisturized and slid into a pair of lightweight Capri pants and a flowy pink top. I'd chosen it for its simplicity and because I knew it drove Mick wild when he had to undress me.

I took out ingredients for beef teriyaki, and I froze at a sound in the back of the house. The kitchen was silent because I'd decided another part of the new me would enjoy the silence. Embrace it rather than filling my mind with sound constantly. It could have been raccoons or this far in the desert it could have been possums, but I didn't think critters were out there banging around. Shutting off the lights so I could see outside, I crept closer until I heard the distinct sound of a human thudding. And then

MICK

groaning. Wrapping my shaky hands around the bat beside the door, I lifted it and opened the door slightly. "Who's out there? I have a weapon and I'm not afraid to use it, asshole!" Yeah, that sounded brave even though my heart beat so fast I thought it might have been louder than the wannabe intruder, but my voice never wavered though fear was palpable in my veins.

I heard the slide and thump of an uneven gait. "Who are you?" The voice came from the dark, scratchy as though whoever it was hadn't had water for days.

I thought for a second maybe a lost hiker had wandered my way, but then, that's exactly what a serial killer would want me to think, right? "I don't think so, buddy. You're at my place, who the hell are you? Show yourself, dammit."

"Dagger," he spat on a groan. I'd heard the name before and when I realized who he was, I reached for my phone and flicked on the flashlight.

"Oh hell," I gasped at the sight of him beaten and bloody. "Come in," I urged, but it became clear moving caused him more pain, so I helped him as best I could considering he was a big man. Tall and solid. "Damn, you're heavy. You lift cars instead of weights?"

He tried to laugh and winced for his efforts. "Funny."

"What the hell happened? Does anything feel broken?"

"Nah, my ribs are bruised, though. I'm just busted up and probably in need of a few stitches." Typical man trying to downplay his injuries.

But I knew better, so I put a hand to his chest until he fell onto the bed in one of the guest rooms, taking off his boots, his cut, and his shirts. All three of them. "Shit. What happened to you? Never mind, don't talk. Drink this water while I gather some supplies, and then I'll let Mick know you're here. Should I let Trudy know, too?" I wanted to make her

MICK

my first call, thinking about how tangled up she'd been over his disappearance.

His eyes flashed gratitude behind the blood and bruising. "Not yet, but thanks."

"Lucky for you my dad had a pretty amazing first-aid kit in here," I told him as I finished cleaning up the blood and rinsing out his wounds. "I'm Talon by the way, Magnus was apparently my dad." I shook his hand and got to work disinfecting the wounds and using butterfly bandages for the ones that needed stitches. "Not the prettiest job, but it's done. I'm afraid I'll need to stitch that gash in your head so…whiskey or tequila?"

Dagger smiled, and I imagined that busted lip hurt like hell. "Yes."

I handed him the bottle of Jim Beam and got to work stitching like I had any medical training. "All better," I told him fifteen minutes and ten stitches later, and then I shot off a text to Mick.

I need you. Bring ice. Come alone. ~T

"Thanks for this," he groaned.

"None necessary. Trudy's worried sick, and that's enough for me." My whole body went still at the now familiar roar of big ass motorcycles in the distance. More than one which meant *not* Mick. "Shit. Dagger, get up."

"Give me up, Talon, it's not worth it."

I rolled my eyes at his attempt at chivalry. "Lord save me from chivalrous men. I'm guessing those visitors are looking for you?" He nodded and I scanned the room, thinking of the blueprints I'd found a few weeks ago. "Well it looks like you sought refuge here at the right time." The room sat on a slant like it had been added on later, and right where the roof met the wall I searched for a seam that wasn't visible. "There," I said when I pushed and the wall opened." Get in and don't make a peep. You're injured so don't try to come to my rescue." He wanted to argue so I shoved him in and shut the door, placing the oversized beanbag against it.

MICK

The sounds of the bikes grew closer, and I knew I didn't have much time. Gathering up all the bloody rags and gauze, Dagger's clothes and boots, and all evidence that someone else had been here, I shoved it the hamper in my bathroom and wet my hair before wrapping it in a towel moments before a loud banging sounded at my door.

Stay calm. You can do this. In movies pep talks always seem to work, to push the person into being stronger, and I hoped like hell it'd work for me. Peeking through a side window, I saw that creepy bastard, Toro, on my porch along with someone I'd never seen before. After a long cleansing breath, I picked up the bat, gripping the handle behind the door. "Yes?"

"You here alone," he barked the question at me as though I owed him an answer.

"None of your business. Why are you here?"

"Mick here?" Toro's scowl deepened, and I knew this guy could do serious damage, but I refused to be afraid.

109

"He will be soon." I hoped so at least.

I could tell right away he didn't believe me, but I didn't give a shit. He didn't know me well enough to know I was lying. "No one is here? You haven't seen Dagger?"

"Who?"

"You mind if we look around?" He moved toward me as though my agreement were a foregone conclusion.

"Actually, I do. I don't know you or him, and I'm not in the habit of letting men I don't know into my home. You can wait until Mick gets here or you can go." I gripped the bat tighter in my hands, sensing that soon I would have to use it.

"You cocky bitch, I can't wait to teach you a fucking lesson," he actually sneered like a fucking cartoon villain.

I laughed to cover all traces of the fear that snaked through me at his words. "I'd like to see you

MICK

try." I knew poking the bear was wrong, ill-advised, but I couldn't seem to help myself.

Though I knew what was about to happen because I saw his raised foot, I couldn't move fast enough when he kicked the door, and I stumbled back. Thankfully I still gripped the bat in my hands, making the greasy fucker grin. "Oh, kitty has claws."

"The better to slit your throat with." I grinned back.

He lunged, and I swung the bat hard too hard because it only grazed his elbow which was enough to slow him down so I could get an actual weapon. Like a knife. "Bitch! You'll pay for that," he groaned.

I heard footsteps behind me, and I ran faster to the kitchen, grabbing the closest knife I could reach just as his hand wrapped around my arm. I turned and sliced at him, sending him reeling back with a roar of pain. "I'll kill you!" The unknown man grabbed my wrist and banged it hard against the wall until I dropped the knife, his other hand twisting around my hair and locking me in his grasp.

Toro spat, "But first, I think I'll teach you a lesson on how bitches are supposed to act."

I swallowed my fear, refusing to show any outward signs to this bastard. I fought against the other man's grasp, trying to work myself free. "The only way you can get any is to take it by force. Another limp dick," I spat seconds before his fist landed hard on the side of my face. My head lurched backward into the man's chest with a resounding thud, but I remained resilient and placed a smile on my face as blood filled my mouth. "Big man," I groaned.

"I don't care what you think, slut, but after tonight you won't take a piss without thinking of me." Toro edged closer, rage blazing in his eyes. "Fucking bitch," he yelled when I raked my nails down his face. "I can't wait to tear you up." He punched me hard, and my legs buckled. The other man tightened his arms around me, but I let my weight fall heavy against him. "Let's see how bad Mick wants you with a fucked up face." He trailed the blade of a knife down

MICK

my jaw with a creepy smile. "Or when you've been fucked so hard you can't sit, can't piss."

Bile rose up in my throat. Fear and adrenaline had me, but I swallowed it down because I could hear the little kick up of gravel outside and I knew, I hoped at least, that meant Mick would soon be here. "Oh yeah? You'd better get that bat then because I doubt I'd feel anything otherwise."

I knew I'd pushed him too far when his face twisted in unspeakable madness, and he raised his hand to strike me again. But the blow didn't land because he was knocked to the ground.

"Mick!" He sat on top of Toro and landed blow after blow. The other man let me go and went after my man. "Mick," I yelled again, but he was too consumed by his rage.

Reaching for the bat, I lifted it over my head and brought it down across the unknown man's back with a satisfying *thwack*. "Mick, stop!"

The sound of flesh knocking the shit out of flesh stopped, and he looked over his shoulder. "Babe, you all right?" He was at my side in a moment, stroking my face, rage building at the sight of the blood and the bruises I was sure had already begun to form on both sides of my face. "I should have gotten here sooner."

"I'm a little banged up, but I'm fine. Your *friends* figured they could come in and search my house without permission, and then thought they'd take a piece of me for their efforts." I knew the blame didn't lie with Mick, but these guys were *his* guys and that made it feel too personal.

His expression darkened and he stood over both men, bloody and groaning. "Church tonight at midnight. It's the only reason you motherfuckers aren't dead right now."

I kind of wished they both were dead as my heart pounded furiously in my chest, and a chill washed over my body. Teeth chattering, I watched

MICK

Mick kick them out of my house, which I feared may never feel like my home again.

Chapter Eight

Mick

If I hadn't been sure about my feelings for Talon before, charging into her house and seeing one of the prospects holding her while Toro got ready to hit her again had brought it all home to me. She meant everything to me, and I had come close to killing a member of my club for her. That was scary shit, but not as scary as what they would have done if I'd gone straight to the clubhouse as I planned. "Darlin', tell me you're all right. Please."

She cupped my jaw more lovingly than I deserved. "I'm shaken up and in pain but okay. They aren't why I called, though." Slowly she rose from the sofa, and I followed her down the hall where the bedrooms were located.

"What's going on? I need to get out of here because some serious shit is going down tonight." I didn't mean to be an asshole after what happened to her, but we finally had the evidence we needed to present to the club.

"Trust me," she said, and I wanted to yell and scream, to go fuck someone up because one silver eye had started to swell and the other had blood creeping in.

"I do."

I guess that satisfied her because she moved that ugly ass beanbag chair that Magnus loved and pressed on the wall until it popped open. "All clear," she groaned and stepped back.

Dagger stepped out looking like he'd been on the losing end of a beat down. "Holy shit, brother, what happened to you?"

"Toro and Wags," he groaned as he stood, leaning on Talon who'd moved in to assist him to the bed. "They're into some bad shit."

MICK

"Yeah, I know. You showed up just in time for Church tonight."

He grinned, but I could see how much pain he was in. "Your girl patched me up. Magnus has a kid, what a kick." Then his gaze finally settled on her again. "What the fuck happened?"

"Your buddies wanted to come in and look for you. I said no."

"Shit, Talon, I'm sorry." He looked so full of regret that any anger I had about him not helping vanished. "I didn't hear shit."

"Thick walls," she said and left the room, returning moments later with a bottle of water and her phone. "Can I let Trudy know you're alive and well? She's worried sick."

"No," he barked angrily. "When this is all over I'll get home to her." His voice softened. "She'll try to come to me now, and it's not safe."

"Fine. There's a truck in the garage, but I'm guessing you know that," she said to me, her eyes no longer full of light and happiness.

I hated that this shit had touched her so closely, too fucking closely. "I do," I finally answered and leaned down to press a kiss to her mouth. "I'm sorry this happened, but I swear I'll make it up to you." I took her mouth again because I couldn't help it. Because she was everything to me. Because I could. "You truly are something special."

She grinned and winced, placing a hand against her bruised and swollen face. "I'm glad you think so, Mick, because I'm sure." She looked up at me, and what I could see of her silver eyes sparkled with love. I just hoped I could be worthy of a woman like her.

"Good to know." I kissed her again, this time longer and hotter, full of meaning before stepping back and helping Dagger to the garage. "Talon?" I turned to where she stood in the doorway.

"Yeah?"

MICK

"I love you, too."

She smiled, and her skin flushed prettily. "Be safe, guys. Come back to me, Mick."

"Always." I meant those words with everything inside of me. I would get the club back on the right track and then I'd come back to my woman and make her mine.

※ ※ ※

"You sure you want to do this, Mick?"

I looked at my President, my leader, and gave him a sharp nod. I more than wanted to do this, I needed to do this shit. "Fuck yeah, I'm sure. You saw what they did to Dagger, and you saw the footage, not to mention what they did to Talon." Then a thought occurred to me. "Are you cool with them going behind your back to do this shit? Pocketing a shit ton of cash that should go to the club?"

His expression darkened, but when he answered with a short, "No," relief flooded my body.

I knew I was being a prick and letting my mouth run away, but Rod didn't seem to get how bad this was for him. For all of us really, but the challenge of his leadership could be dangerous for him. "If this shit comes back, it'll be on the club not just Toro and Wags. I don't want Talon or Minx or anyone's ol' ladies to pay for their shit. They pay enough for ours."

"Yeah, yeah. I got it, Mick, and I'm with you. Let's do this shit." He clapped my back and slid open the doors of the Church of CAOS. It's where we held all of our important meetings, voted on club matters from stripping members of their tags to removing tattoos and welcoming new prospects. For us this room was as sacred as any other church.

Roddick took his seat at the head of the table and removed the bandana that kept his black hair tied back. The silver outlaw gavel in his hand as he looked at the men already assembled. The empty seats belonged to the traitors whose fates we would decide tonight.

MICK

Toro and Wags strolled in, all smiles despite the ass kicking they took earlier. I looked forward to taking these motherfuckers down. Especially the prick who'd laid hands on Talon. "Looks like the gang's all here." He smirked and took his seat to Rod's right.

"Sit down!" Rod's bark echoed in the room, drawing the attention of everyone. Those still standing sat except Toro. Defiant to the fucking end.

Toro finally sat, leaning back in a casual stance that underscored the tension in his face. "Is this 'cause Mick got his panties in bunch? You can't blame me for wanting a piece of that fine ass. Would've gotten it too if you weren't such a pussy."

"Big talk for a man who got his face bashed in. Didn't realize rape was a part of CAOS these days," I spat and let the room absorb those words. "I got the bruises you put on her as proof. Want to deny it so we can settle this outside?"

He paled, but the bastard refused to back down. "Anytime."

"Enough," Rod growled, his patience obviously at its breaking point. "Church is now is session. We need to talk about some of the rumors I've been hearing and frankly I don't fucking like." He outlined the basics, that club members are providing unsanctioned protection for shit we don't deal in.

"Probably just a few assholes jealous because they're broke." Toro grinned, but I could see the lines tightening around his eyes and mouth.

Rod looked him head on. "So, you're telling me that you aren't one of the men providing protection so the Mexican Devils can get drugs across the border? What about the Aces & Spades? The Star Fuckers?"

"I don't know what you're talking about. You have something to say, say it."

Rod nodded and looked around the room. "Does every voting member in the room know the penalty for stealing money from the club?"

MICK

Everyone nodded because we all fucking knew.

"And double dealing," Rod added with a glare.

We all nodded again.

"And what about going against the club?"

We all banged against the table knowing that the penalty for that particular sin was a date with the Outlaw.

"Good. Then let's get down to business." The flat screen on the wall flickered on, and the grainy video footage Cash and I shot began to play. After a few grumbles the room fell silent, watching Toro shake hands with Lazarus, take cash from Lazarus, and lead him and his men to a safe house that belonged to the Star Fuckers.

"This is bullshit!" Toro stood and banged his hands on the table in fake ass outrage. He marched to the door but found two prospects standing guard and turned back to Roddick. "You know I wouldn't do that."

Yeah, that fucker was afraid now.

Rod stood up, every fucking inch the battle-hardened President he was. We needed. "I thought that too, but then I spoke to Lazarus. And Dante and Xiao. They all told me about these deals they thought were brokered with my okay. Funny, Toro, I don't recall any of these fucking deals."

Toro paled while Rocky and Wagman remained silent. No one knew who else was involved yet, and those assholes kept their mouths shut. "We did the heavy lifting, so we earned that money," he shot back, full of defiance.

Rod stared him down for a long moment, probably thinking of all the shit they'd been through together. Those two had been around for decades, had each other's backs for a long time, and this kind of betrayal had to sting. He banged the Outlaw gavel five times in honor of the five founding members. "Call to a vote on VP Toro for stealing club funds. For brokering deals against club interests. For killing a fellow Outlaw."

MICK

"I did *not* kill Magnus! But the muthafucker'd still be alive if he'd just kept the produce comin' in the way it was. We had a deal!" The fear in his eyes told me that was exactly what he'd done, but my guess was, he had the prospect do it.

"Really, because I have three affidavits that say you did." Rod's gaze never left Toro's, whose own gaze flickered to two of his accomplices. "Vote on expulsion, Dagger."

"Aye." His palms banged forcefully on the table.

"Vote, Mick," Rod spoke with steely determination.

"Aye."

"Vote, Baz."

"Aye."

"Vote, Torch."

"Aye, motherfucker!" Our enforcer was a crazy bastard, and he'd be the one to administer CAOS justice if it came to that.

"Aye," Rod said forcefully. "Toro expelled from CAOS. Torch, get the gun."

Wild eyes looked around the room. "You haven't voted on that yet!"

Rod smiled, but there was no amusement there. "No. First, we get rid of your ink, and then we decide if you meet the Outlaw."

I stood toe to toe with Toro and cut off his VP patch, tossing it on the table while Dagger removed his cut. It gave me great pleasure to be the one to strip that bastard of his title. Of his club. "Prospect, take him to the south building," I said with a grin.

"Now we vote again," Rod said, and we went through the same thing with Wagman and then Rocky. "It's unanimous, Rocky and Wagman expelled from CAOS."

MICK

Every remaining member banged their hands on the table, all shouting, "Outlaw! Outlaw!"

Rod stood and looked around the room while they were escorted to the south building along with the prospect who helped them. "Now we vote on Outlaw or Mercy for our former members." Everyone quieted and turned to Rod because this vote was a big fucking deal. The Outlaw vote was rare, even in a club full of outlaws. We were all former military and we knew loyalty, had it drilled into us from an early age. All capable of taking a life, we tried hard not to. "Mercy vote."

A quick glance around the room told me what I suspected. Toro's crimes were too heinous to warrant mercy. No hands were in the air.

"Outlaw vote."

One hand went up and the others pounded a fist on the table, all the way around the fucking table. "Toro meets the Outlaw," Rod said with a grin.

Torch, the crazy motherfucker that he was, brought out two bottles of the good shit. Whiskey bottles were passed around, the mood somber and jubilant. We hated that any CAOS member had to meet the Outlaw, but we were all happy to get rid of the toxic parts of the club. "We ain't leaving 'til the bottles are empty," he yelled and let out his signature howl.

"Looks like we have a few seats to fill," Rod said, calling attention back to Church. We were down one prospect, but there were plenty of men on the other side of that door we could trust to be loyal and honest. Who'd been to battle with us and come out the other side. "Mick, I want you as my VP, all in favor."

Everyone was on board, but I looked to Dagger who didn't seem to have a problem with it. "I'm happy with my weapons." He grinned, his smile streaked with filth and blood.

MICK

I grinned back, still smiling like a giddy teenager when Torch removed my Treasurer patch and gave me the VP patch. "Congrats, brother."

"Thanks."

"Get Cash in here," Roddick ordered when we voted him in as club Secretary. "Rich, too," he said of our newest Road Captain.

I smiled, looking around the table at our newly assembled club, whole and happy. We had a long night ahead of us, and though I was instrumental in everything that would happen before the sun came up, all I really wanted to do was go home and crawl into bed with Talon.

MICK

Chapter Nine

Talon

I didn't think I would ever get sick of the view from my back deck. Early mornings like this were my favorite. A slight chill in the air as the sun rose at her leisure, slowing warming everything she touched. Rays of pink and orange dotted the sky, making the world come alive before my eyes. Maybe it had to do with the news I'd gotten two days ago that had given me the rosy glow of life. Of Brently. Of love.

Yeah, I was also deeply in love with Mick, and though he said it last month before all the shit with CAOS went down, he hasn't said it since which made me think he'd said it because he thought there was a good chance he wouldn't come back to me. But he had, and he'd spent nearly every single night since in my bed. In my home. We were solid. Together.

And I had news to share with him. Big news. But I had no clue how he'd react. Hence the sitting on my deck watching the sun come up. He was due back today from a trip to Colorado to deliver a few custom bikes, and I'd spent the past twenty-four hours trying to gather my courage. While I thought Mick might be happy about my news, I couldn't be sure. I mean, I thought Damon and I were solid until I found him fucking my so-called best friend on my kitchen table. So, what the hell did I know about men?

But I had high hopes and positive thinking and all that crap. If things didn't go as planned, I had a backup plan that included staying in Brently and running the diner. Maybe even putting up a greenhouse on my property. Anything to make my life normal. *Our* life normal.

The sun rose high in the sky, and I pushed off the cushioned Adirondack and went into the house to make some lemon ginger tea and biscuits. Coffee

MICK

would be sorely missed, but giving it up was worth it. While the tea brewed, I made breakfast and sat down with my tablet, going over new menu additions. I liked the greasy spoon feel of Black Betty, but I figured by changing it up we could increase the revenue as much as was possible in this small town. Nothing too dramatic, I'd read and watched enough small town stories to know change was received better in small doses.

"And here I was expecting a coming home party."

I froze and looked up at the big gorgeous man with flaming red hair and a scruffy beard that almost hid the seductive grin he wore. His emerald eyes sparkled with amusement. "I'm here, isn't that enough of a party?"

"Depends. What's this party of one entail?"

That lazy grin always made my pussy clench, and this morning was no different. "Well, you're here so it's a party of two. Technically."

"I like where this party is headed."

"I thought you might." Mick had an insatiable sexual appetite. It always amazed me just how many times he could go in a night and how he was always ready for me. I stood and leaned against the table. "So, what kind of party were you hoping for?"

He dropped down in the chair across from me and grabbed a slice of bacon from my plate. Before he bit down on it, his stomach rumbled and we both laughed. "I guess I'll need actual food." He leaned back with his trademark predatory grin. "And here I'd planned to eat you first."

A shiver shot through me that I couldn't stop, and he laughed. "Well I might taste good, but I doubt you'll get much sustenance."

"Making you the perfect dessert."

Damn this man and how hard I'd fallen for him. "So…breakfast?"

"To start."

MICK

I loved cooking for Mick. Unlike Damon, he appreciated my downhome cooking and didn't require me to cook sophisticated food I'd never eaten before. Not that I didn't like to experiment, I did, but at my own comfort level. A quick meal of bacon, eggs and toast and Mick was happy. "Here you go."

"Thanks, babe." He pulled me down for a kiss that stole my breath and wet my panties, which made me think of the thing I really needed to tell him. But I wasn't ready yet.

"Eat." I sat and finished my own food, thinking of how much we seemed like an old married couple, sitting here quietly eating breakfast like we'd known each other forever. When we hadn't. "Can you believe it's been just four months since I met you? It feels like longer." Abby and Damon and Chicago seemed like a lifetime ago because I'd jumped into my new life with both feet.

He laughed. "I don't know if that's supposed to be a good thing or a bad thing."

"It's great. I feel like you've been in my heart for as long as I can remember." He didn't speak for a long time as he made quick work of his breakfast, but I saw the different emotions play out on his face. "I love you, Mick."

"I love you too, baby, and if we're gonna get mushy, I think I should be holding you." Since his arms were my favorite place to be, I went willingly to him, and he scooped me in his arms and settled us on the sofa. "I never thought I could love anybody as much as I love you."

I needed to hear those words, and they caused a reaction throughout my body. I felt emotional, turned on, fulfilled and so full of love I thought I might burst with it. But sitting here in his lap, I felt something long and hard pressing against my ass. "I didn't think I wanted love again, but I find myself loving everything about you. Your smile." I kissed him slow and sensual. "Your heart. Your kindness." I laid a hand over his heart. "I love the feel of you in my

MICK

hand. My pussy." I leaned forward and whispered, "My mouth."

He groaned and stood. "I love it when you talk dirty to me. Your sweet little mouth saying nasty shit to me gets me so fuckin' hard." He walked us down the hall and to the bedroom. "I need to rinse off two straight days of road, and when I get out I want you spread across the bed naked and dripping for me."

"Not a problem," I groaned, my gaze riveted to every inch of skin he revealed. I felt moisture flood my thighs, and I squeezed them tight. "I'll be right here. Warming up."

"No. Mine." He disappeared into the bathroom and I listened to the shower start, picturing his naked body slick with water. I had to tamp down my arousal because I needed to tell him the news. I couldn't make love with him again before he knew.

Could I?

My body was hot and heavy, pulsing with desire that warred with my need to do the right thing.

But when he stepped from the bathroom—totally naked—with a hungry look in his eyes, I knew I needed just a taste. In case it was the last I had. "Mr. Vice President, you are looking mighty delicious. And so, so far away."

He walked to the side of the bed and stood there, staring at my naked form. "I'm closer now."

I reached out and wrapped my hand around the hard length of his cock and squeezed. Tugged. He groaned, and I leaned forward until I could wrap my mouth around him instead. His taste was pure maleness. Earthy and musky and delicious. Closing my eyes, I sucked him hard, took him deep, and made love to his cock with my mouth. Every groan he released, every muttered curse word made my pussy flood.

"Talon," he groaned, but I already felt it. He grew harder and then the hot jets shot into my mouth and down my throat while I licked and sucked slower and slower. "Talon." He held my head as his hips jerked a few more times before he pulled out and collapsed beside me. "I love your mouth, almost as much as I love you."

I laughed. "High praise considering I just sucked you off."

His body shook with laughter and before I knew what happened, he grabbed my thighs and lifted me until I was straddling his head. "And you did a great job, baby. Now it's time for dessert. Hold on."

I held on to the headboard while his tongue darted in and out of my pussy, making stars explode behind my eyes. But when his tongue went flat and wide as it licked me from clit to opening, I held on tighter as my hips began to move in a slow grinding motion against his mouth. "Mick. Fuck yeah, Mick."

"Yeah, that's it, baby, fuck my face."

His words more than the sharp smack to my ass spurred me on, widening my stance and moving my hips against him faster and harder as my orgasm began to build. One hand reached down to hold his head, and I moved even faster, grounding against him as pleasure shot out of every pore. Light and fire and electricity flew out of me as I cried out his name over and over. My hips slowed but his tongue didn't, wrapping around my clit and lifting me up once again before I had a chance to get away from his magical mouth. "That was so dirty. And so fuckin' hot," I panted while he laughed beside me. "That's just what I needed."

"Glad to be of service, darlin'."

I turned so we were face to face and rested my hands on his chest. He was beautiful and masculine. And perfect. "We need to talk."

He sighed and flung an arm over his face so I couldn't see him. "I know, Talon. I promise we'll talk soon, but I don't have all of my shit together yet."

"What?"

"You're ready for the next step, right? That's what all the talk was of being together for four months and the best blow job of my life, wasn't it? So

MICK

you could butter me up before telling me you're ready to move forward."

I pulled back. "You think *that's* what I was doing?"

"I do and I appreciate it, but it's not necessary. I told you Talon, I love you. You're it for me."

"But?"

"But a man has to do this kind of thing in his own time." He sounded so resigned to commitment that I almost had to rethink telling him. But I wasn't a coward. "Just because you're ready today doesn't mean I'm ready to do it today."

"Oh my God, will you please shut up!" I stood and reached for my robe, suddenly feeling chilled.

"Just sayin`."

"Stop saying anything! I wasn't asking you for a ring, I just wanted one last memory before I told you I'm pregnant!" I stepped over his clothes and mine on my way to the bathroom and slammed the door behind me. "Jerk!"

His knock on the door was insistent as though he were trying to break it down. "You're pregnant, Talon? For real?"

"Yes!" I smacked the door angrily.

"Seriously?"

"Nine weeks. Serious, Mick."

"Open the door."

I unlocked the door and slid against the tub. When the door opened, I refused to look up at him. "I know it's soon. If you're not ready for this then you're not ready, Mick. It wouldn't be the first time I had to handle things on my own."

"Of course I'm ready. I'm happier than hell about this."

"You are? Because you didn't sound all that happy just a few minutes ago."

"Fuck yeah, I am. Get up." He lifted me up before I could even process his words and set me on my feet. "Get dressed."

MICK

"Mick, what the hell is going on?" He turned me toward the door and pushed my shoulders until I started to move.

"Get dressed and meet me in the living room. Hurry." He strode out, leaving me wondering what the hell just happened.

***

Mick

"You kind of stole my thunder, babe, but I can improvise. Never let it be said that I'm a man who can't think on his feet." As the bike came to a stop on the overlook I took her to the first time we fucked, my heart raced so loudly I could hear it over the roar of my bike. *Pregnant.* I'm going to be a dad.

"I think you're pretty good at thinking on your feet, but I'm confused about why we're here." Big silver eyes smiled up at me while tiny ebony wisps blew in the breeze.

"I know you are, and that's okay. By the time we get back on my bike you won't be."

"Okay."

I grabbed her hand, and we looked out over Brently below and the clubhouse in the distance just off the interstate ramp and beyond that, Tacapeo. "That first night up here with you changed my life for the better. I hadn't realized that I was even looking for someone to share my life with until you refused to stay out of mind. I couldn't get enough of you. I couldn't stop thinking about you."

"Mick," she whispered, all breathy and sexy before bringing my hand to her mouth and pressing a kiss to the center of my palm.

"Talon, you give of yourself so freely. Your heart and your body, your laughter. Everything. You showed me I could live this life and have a woman like you by my side. You are everything I didn't even know I was looking for, and I know I won't ever be happy without you beside me. I love you."

"I love you too, baby. More than anything."

MICK

"I love you, too, and our baby. Will you marry me?"

She gave an amused grin. "And be your ol' lady for life?"

I smirked at her playfulness. "Hell yeah."

"In that case, fuck yeah, I'll marry you." She jumped into my arms and wrapped her body around mine, kissing me like her life depended on it.

I held her tight and vowed to myself, as we kissed under the sun, that I'd never let her go. "A baby and a wife, must be my lucky day."

"Must be."

I felt like I was forgetting something but then I remembered. "Can't have a fiancée without a ring, right?" I'd picked it up in Denver on my way out of town. The ring was simple—platinum band with an emerald cut pink diamond surrounded by smaller white ones—and perfectly Talon. I slid it on her finger and she gasped, tears shimmered in those big, trusting silver eyes. "One more time. Talon, will you marry me?"

"It's beautiful, Mick. I'm yours and I can't wait to be your wife."

Thank fuck. Looks like a guy like me can also get his happily ever after, too.

MICK

Epilogue

Talon ~ *3 months later*

"Damn, girl, you move fast. I'm impressed." Minx grinned at me and bumped my shoulder. "A baby on the way and a husband."

I rubbed my slightly rounded belly and shook my head at her tone. "Not a husband yet, just a fiancé. That's why we're celebrating with our engagement party here tonight." It was more like a backyard barbecue because no one here stood on ceremony, and honestly, I'd been craving barbecue all the time lately. With the weather slightly cooling, I'd been taking advantage of my craving with barbecue chicken, ribs, burgers and even sausages. It was getting ridiculous and if I didn't get a handle on it, I'd gain fifty pounds before the baby got here. We'd opted for an engagement barbecue on First Street in front of the diner. Mick wanted it at the club, but I thought after everything that had happened we should make it a Brently thing. Besides, while I supported his club membership, I still felt a little weird being there.

"Either way, Talon, you're the envy of every *pass-around* here." I knew what she meant because I'd gotten more than a few nasty glares since I'd arrived. Especially Janine who'd been making snide remarks for the past few weeks.

"I can't worry about them when I have a wedding to plan and a baby to get ready for. Do you know anything about weddings or babies, because I don't?" I hadn't been around babies much in my life other than at amusement parks and restaurants. Not enough to actually take care of one. I was terrified.

Minx laughed and hopped up on the stool beside me, looking amazing in short denim shorts, a plain white tee that hugged her gorgeous breasts and her ever-present cowboy boots. I wondered how

MICK

many pairs she had. "I know more about babies than weddings. Somewhere in the world I have a kid brother and sister." She said it so casually, but I could see the wistfulness in her eyes. She missed her family.

"Does that mean you don't want to be my maid of honor?" She was my only close friend and since she hadn't ever fucked Mick, I figured we were solid.

She turned to me, big brown eyes looking so vulnerable I wanted to pull her into a hug. "You want *me* to be your maid of honor? Why?"

"You're my friend. My best friend, and I want you beside me on this important day. You don't want to do it?" Tears welled up in my eyes, and I was firmly blaming it on pregnancy hormones and not on the fact that she was rejecting me.

She swiped a tear that I pretended not to see and nodded. "No, I do, it's just... Don't you want someone more, I don't know, someone else?"

I wrapped an arm around her. "No, I want you even though you're so fucking hot you'll totally upstage me on my wedding day. I still want you beside me. Say you'll do it."

"I'll do it." She gave me a long hug, and I felt all the pain Minx had been through in her life. I thought I had it hard, but I didn't know shit about hard compared to her experiences. Based on her reaction to something I took as a simple request between friends, I knew it was worse than I could ever imagine. I just hoped one day she'd confide in me about it. "How'd you get me a night off for this shindig?"

"I told Mick that the maid of honor had to be at the engagement party."

"You were so sure I'd agree?"

I barked out a laugh. "No way, but I was hopeful and full of hormones. If that hadn't worked, I would've bribed you with my lasagna. Or tears."

"Your tacos are better," she shot back, sassy smile back in place.

MICK

"Good to know." I cooked a lot these days, and I found it was a good way to get things done around the house, whether it was help in my garden or moving things in the nursery. Mick and Charlie never needed bribing, but I enjoyed cooking for them just the same.

"So, I have something for you, but I don't want you to make a big pregnant deal out of it, okay?"

Minx hated emotions, so I nodded without making any promises. She handed me a tall black and silver box wrapped with a beautiful black bow. I gasped when I lifted the top off and took sight of the shimmery, sparkling black tiara. "It's gorgeous."

"Can't have the VP's ol' lady looking anything but fierce, right?" She smiled as she lifted it out and set it on my head. "It's black rhinestones and Swarovski crystals topped with black pearls."

"Holy crap, Minx, it's amazing. Thank you." I pulled her in and squeezed her tight. "No one has ever gotten me something so cool!"

"You promised."

"I know I did, but I'm pregnant and I can't help it. Deal with it."

"Fine. You're lucky I love you."

"I love you too, Minx." I opened my eyes to see Mick behind her, watching us with a concerned glare. "I'm fine, I promise. Look at Minx's gift."

His gaze flared with heat. "It's nice. Wear it tonight and nothing else?"

"Oh hell," Minx moaned and stomped off.

"I have a killer pair of stilettos that I can only wear if I won't be on my feet all night," I offered with a coy smile.

"Baby, you'll be on your back all night. I might even rub your feet and kiss those little piggy toes. That's a promise."

"Is it too early to leave?"

He laughed and pulled me in close, the way he always did. "Probably, but do you really care?" He

MICK

saw the indecision written on my face. "We have all night, darlin'."

I looked up at him and grinned. "We have the rest of our lives."

***

Mick

My girl looked so fucking beautiful tonight, round with my baby in her belly. Skin flushed in a light sheen that made her look like she was fucking glowing. And man, her tits were bigger and so sensitive it took nothing at all to get her going. "You look beautiful tonight. Did I tell you that?"

With a sassy smile, she nuzzled my neck as I inhaled her hair. Honeysuckle. "Only about a thousand times. Thanks, and you're looking mighty fine as well."

I'd opted for a lightweight olive green button up with my jeans and boots. The way she looked at me right now, like she wanted to drop down and gobble me up, had my dick growing hard against my jeans. If anyone would have told me that I'd be so turned on by a pregnant woman, I would've told them they were out of their fucking mind. But my woman did it for me. In a big damn way. "Thanks, darlin', but don't go sayin' shit like that or my fiancée might slap the shit outta ya. She's feisty like that."

"Yeah, she is. Don't you forget it." She adjusted her tiara and puckered up for a kiss. "Have you seen Charlie lately? She left a message saying she couldn't make it tonight and that she was going away for a while."

"She stopped by the service station on her way out of town, said to tell you she's not abandoning you. She needs to clear her head and think about everything. She'll be back in a couple weeks." I saw tears building in her eyes, and they gutted me. "If you need any extra help, babe, you know I've got you. Right?"

MICK

"I know, and I'll be fine. I just hate that she's going through all of this. I mean, I kind of feel what she does right now and I never knew Magnus, but she's loved him for years and years, and the people she thought were her friends killed him."

"You're kind of too good to be true, you know?"

She shrugged and pressed her nose to my chest and inhaled. "You smell like a dream. Every time I sniff you I get all kinds of wet."

"Damn, baby, you keep saying things like that, and I'll have to take you behind the diner and have my way with you."

Talon backed away from me, a teasing grin on her face. "Behind the diner like I'm some hussy?" She frowned and shook her head, eyes alight with amusement. "No, I have a slightly uncomfortable two-seater in my office that I think will be much more comfortable for both of us."

In one step, I was in front of her, one hand low on her back and the other palming the spot where our child grew. "I like the way you think." I slanted my mouth over hers and she opened up right away, slicking her tongue across mine in a naughty way that had me picking her up and walking straight into the diner. "Can we use some of that whipped cream you keep in the fridge?"

She laughed, skin flushing at the thought of what we'd done when she brought home a way too large bowl of fresh whipped cream. "I've created a monster!"

"Hell yeah, baby, a trouser monster!"

Fingers hooked into my belt loops, she pulled me through the diner and down the hall where her tiny ass office was located. "You know, Mick, I love you. I really, really do. But I think tonight, I'm going to have my way with you."

I smiled while she undressed me, her slick pink tongue stuck out of the corner, deep in concentration as she undid my belt, then my button

MICK

before lowering the zipper. "Damn, woman, I don't know if I could love you more than I do right now."

"Let's see if I can change that."

Looking down into those sparkling silver eyes filled with love, I knew every day we spent together would fill my heart with more love for her. For our baby and however many other babies we made together. She was a one of a kind girl, and I was pretty fucking sure Magnus had sent her here just for me.

Thanks, Magnus, you old dog.

~The End.~

Acknowledgements

Thank you! I love you all and thank you for making my books a success!! I appreciate each and every one of you.

Thanks to all of my beta readers, street teamers, ARC readers and Facebook fans. Y'all are THE BEST!

And a huge very special thanks to my wonderful PA, Silla. Without you, I'd be a hot mess! With you, I'm a hot mess, but without your keen sense of organization and skills, I'd be a burny fiery inferno of hot mess!! Thank you!

And a very special thanks to my editor, Silla Webb (who sometimes has to work all through the night! See HOT MESS above!) Thank you for making my words make sense.

Copyright © 2016 BookBoyfriends Publishing
LLC KB WINTERS

KB Winters

About The Author

KB Winters has an addiction to caffeine, tattoos and hard-bodied alpha males. The men in her books are very sexy, protective and sometimes bossy, her ladies are…well…bossier!

Living in sunny Southern California, the embarrassingly hopeless romantic writes every chance she gets!

You can connect with KB on [Facebook (https://www.facebook.com/kbwintersauthor)](https://www.facebook.com/kbwintersauthor) and [Twitter (http://twitter.com/kbwintersauthor)](http://twitter.com/kbwintersauthor)!